The Sisters of Dragoness:

QUAGMIRE'S REVENGE

Alisa Guttadauro

Cover design by Jeanine Henning
Book design by Maureen Cutajar (www.gopublished.com)

ISBN-13: 978-1688897137

To Sammy Abujaja, a strong warrior, great friend, and genuinely wonderful person. Although you were taken away from us too soon, you will forever remain in our hearts. Fly with the Angels Sammy, you are surely one of them.

Part One

"Careful with the trident!" hissed Raven to her sister Ruby. "Thanks a lot," Ruby snapped back, "I nearly dropped it!" The magical trident was handed down to the sisters from their father Edrical, a wizard, who was killed by the wicked dragon Quagmire, some years ago. The girls lived in Dragoness, a land in the kingdom of Equonicous, which was once a peaceful place for all of its inhabitants. A tear fell from Ruby's eye as she thought of her father. The trident, which was made of steel, had a birthstone on each of its three points. The first stone was an amethyst which represented the girl's mother's birthstone. The second was Raven's birthstone which was an emerald, and the third, a Ruby, which happened to be Ruby's birthstone. There was only one stone missing, which should have been at the handle of the trident, and it was the most powerful of all the stones, a black onyx. Without it, the weapon could not perform to its fullest potential. The magical trident was used for protection against hostile enemies, but, at the time of Quagmire's attack, the trident had been stolen by an evil sorceress, who was Quagmire's mistress. The girl's mother, Willow, had destroyed the sorceress, who was named Iniquitous, with the help of Adorna, an expert swordswoman, and the girl's godmother. The Feelers, who were empaths, held magical powers of sight, and spell weaving. They contributed to the downfall of Iniquitous, but unfortunately, by the time they recovered the trident, Quagmire's strength had vastly increased, and Edrical lost the battle with the vile creature. The kingdom consisted of four lands, Beauteous, which was where King Edgeworth and Queen Primrose held reign, Shimrock Mountain, which was a huge mountain that sparkled like silver and held many inhabitants from gnomes to mums, and every magical creature in between, Wickardia, which was where the enchanted wickets lived and made all of the kingdom's magical candles from their own ear wax, and Dragoness, which was where the sisters resided. There was a fifth land, Ralliant, but it was taken over by the evil Murk brothers, who were twins and minions of the dark dragon Quagmire. Ralliant which was once a beautiful land of mermaids, mermen, and shimmering blue waters was now dark, dank, and murky. Re-named, 'Murk Island,' by the Murk brothers, it was a land of dread and destruction. The Murk brothers inhabited the land after they fled with Quagmire. Except for Murk Island, each land had a unique beauty of its own, and was guarded by the people who lived there. Once Edrical was killed, and the Murk brothers took Quagmire to hide him at Murk Island, all of the occupants of the kingdom suffered from a disadvantage; they weren't as powerful as they once were. It was like something in the atmosphere changed and they had to work even harder to cast spells or use defensive magic. It seemed like those hideous Murk brothers, Nefari and Querd, had some help because even with the inhabitants of the kingdom being powered down so to speak, they should have been able to conquer the brothers. Those two were always able to sneak around and wreak havoc, whenever they wanted to, plus they have kept Quagmire hidden well the past couple of years. Quagmire, which was the name the Murk brothers gave him, when they had stolen the dragon's egg before he was born, was supposed to be brought up in Dragoness, but unfortunately, the brothers found out the hiding place of the three dragons' eggs and were able to obtain one, before anyone caught on. There were still two eggs hidden somewhere in the kingdom, and if the brothers found them first, they'd be one step closer to taking over the whole kingdom.

Raven took one look at her younger sister, and immediately felt guilty. "I'm sorry Red," Raven's nickname for her sister who's hair looked like fire, "I…I It's…" Ruby wiped her eyes, "I know, it's all we have left of him." Raven and Ruby Shadowstone, lived with their mother, Willow, in Dragoness, a world of magic, alchemy, sorcery, and dragons. Their father, Edrical Shadowstone, was a great wizard, who died a hero's death trying to save their world from the corrupt and loathsome savages who insisted on destroying all that was good. Raven who had just turned eighteen had fully come into her powers, but she still had to work extra hard to use them because of the attack they all suffered years ago, making everyone's talents less potent. Telekinesis was her main talent, which she had been practicing for the past two years. Her beautiful dark hair, which attributed to her mother naming her Raven, was always worn in a long plait. She said it kept her hair off her face, especially helpful if she was ever caught in combat. Her voluminous green eyes were warm, but weary because she was always worried about something, especially her younger sister. Ruby wore her long, radiant red mane loose. She said it made her feel free and unfettered. Her big dark brown eyes were mischievous and sparkled when she laughed, which could be a good thing or a bad thing, depending on if she could control her powers. Ruby learned about her strongest power by accident one day while she was having an argument with her friend Gregor, who was a young wizard, and a constant prankster.

She was working on a spell one day and Gregor had hidden

one of the ingredients she needed to complete it. Ruby became so angry at Gregor that a fire bolt shot out of her eye and almost singed his ear off. It only came out of her right eye so her mother had her wear an eye patch over that eye until they figured out how to control Ruby's newly found gift. Since Ruby was only sixteen, her magic wasn't fully developed yet, and sometimes her temper grew as hot as her flaming red hair. Both girls were beautiful in their own way, as was their mother Willow who was flaxen haired, and fair. Their father, Edrical had had dark hair like Raven. Willow was a witch, and a very good one at that, but the people of dragoness had to be aware of evil still because although Iniquitous was vanquished, Quagmire had disappeared vowing his revenge before he retreated.

Ruby hugged her sister as they both placed their father's trident in the special chest, their mother made for it, out of tree bark and enchanted stones. The girls smiled as the scent of lilacs hit their noses. "Mother," they both said at the same time. Their mother always wore lilac perfume; it had been their father's favorite. Willow looked at her daughters and frowned, "Reminiscing again, I see?" Ruby looked down at her feet, and Raven replied, "Nothing of the sort mother, we were discussing what we needed from Serena's." Serena's Potions Shop was where you went to buy what you needed to make potions, and pretty much anything else. It was a special, mystical place and depending on how advanced you were with your magic, certain effects, so to speak, were not available to you. There was a huge room in the back of the store that was used for training, most specifically swordsmanship, with an area for spell casting. Past the training room was a big wooden door which led to a tunnel. The tunnel led passage to the outside into a magnificent, ethereal garden. The garden was protected by an ancient fairy spell to protect the creatures that lived there. The Wickets, who lived in Wickardia, one of the four lands in the Kingdom, were small troll like beings who made enchanted candles out of their ear wax. Normally, that would be gross, but, these were magical trolls, with spellbinding powers, and colorful earwax. The candles were used for various reasons, such as casting spells, lighting the way during travel, and healing purposes. Daily, the delightful creatures would deliver these majestic candles to the forest garden, and would travel back and forth through a secret tunnel. The female wickets all had long beautiful, colorful hair which was always sought after for certain spells. When they had their hair trimmed, the cuttings were saved, tied in bundles with magical twine and stored in protected treasure boxes, by color. The trolls despised loud noises, and often times would wear special ear muffs during training time at Serena's shop. Being that the trolls were expert gardeners, they often would supply Serena with herbs and plants she needed for her potions which they cultivated from the fruitful forest they so loved so much, and looked after. In turn, Serena offered them protection and knowing how much the mystical creatures loved her freshly baked strawberry muffins, she gladly baked extra for them.

The bell on Serena's shop door jingled, and she smiled as she watched Raven and Ruby walk in. The shop was cozy and Serena always had something baking in the quaint back kitchen. One wall in the shop was full of bookshelves housing every magical book you could want, and the other held beautifully hand blown glass goblets, bowls, and mugs. In the glass case by the register, there were handmade charms and jewelry. With the smell of muffins baking and the delightful atmosphere, the potions shop was a comforting place to hang out. "What will it be today, young ladies?" Serena asked mischievously. "I have training today with aunt Adorna," Raven said excitedly. Ruby stomped her foot, "I don't understand why I cannot train too!"

"When you learn not to scorch anyone's ears off, then maybe you'll be ready," smirked Adorna, who seemingly appeared out of nowhere. Serena stifled a smirk and pretended to count the new gemstones she received that morning, while Raven giggled. Ruby's eye started to twitch, but she remained in control, and just exhaled loudly, frowning. "Ah, very good, very good!" praised Adorna, "Keep that up, and you'll be ready in no time!" Despite being annoyed, Ruby began to smile, "So you were just testing me?" she questioned her aunt. "Adorna laughed lightly, "Yes my little robin and you passed with flying colors. Do not be envious of your sister, your time will come. In the mean while, get a hold on this fire power of yours, which is of great importance. We will discuss it at another time, have patience. With that the expert swordswoman retreated to the back to wait for Raven. Ruby sighed, "Good luck today Raven, I'll see you later." "Thank you Red!" Raven replied, as she ran to the back to start her sword training. Serena smiled, "I see you have a list with you." Ruby started to open her mouth when all of a sudden there was a bright flash of light and the store started to shake. Glass goblets and containers flew off the shelves and broke. Ruby screamed, and Serena yelled, "Get down!" Ruby ran behind the counter with Serena just as a big puff of black smoke filled the room.

Serena held tightly to Ruby, and told her to keep her head down. When the smoke dissipated, hovering above the floor was a gorgon like bird, with three heads. It was hideous, and emitted a foul stench. The creature clicked its long yellow claws together and hissed, each mouth sharing a part of the sentence, "Beware of once was, for it will be again, the tides are turning, my wrath will begin. Many will suffer, vengeance is mine, all will be clear in due time!" A loud whistling sound pierced the air just then as Adorna's dagger came flying at the grotesque creature who cried out and tried to avoid the hit. Raven, who was standing beside her aunt, looked at the sword behind the counter on the wall and sent it flying at the creature while she and Adorna chanted, "Ecru Sonata lagora throosh!" There was a loud thunderous vibration as the evil being vaporized, and then there was silence. Angrily, Adorna said, "Is everyone okay?" Serena, still holding onto Ruby, said in a shaky voice, "What in the world was that!" Ruby, her hand covering her right eye exclaimed, "This is why I need to be trained!" Raven shushed her sister, "Not now Ruby, this is serious!" "Like I don't know that!" retorted Ruby, her eyes flashing. "Girls!" thundered Adorna, "Enough bickering, I think we were just warned that Quagmire is trying to make a return, and if this is the case, not only are we in danger, but so is the whole kingdom. Ruby is right, although she hasn't received all of her powers yet, she will need to be trained. I will have to go speak to Willow, and I'll need both of you girls and Gregor here first thing tomorrow morning."

"Gregor, give me back my bow!" shouted Ruby. Gregor laughed, "Come and get it, if you dare!" "Listen you two," admonished Raven, "Just because aunt Adorna isn't here yet…" "Ah," a voice interrupted, "The children are quarrelling maybe you three should go back to the fairies for kinder lessons." Ruby stomped her foot, and opened her mouth to reply, but Raven put her hand up. "And who might you be sir?" she asked in a curious tone. "My name is Radkiel; I am the royal crop keeper, and an avian wizard." Radkiel smirked at the quizzical looks on the teenagers faces. Then, in a puff of smoke, the wizard was gone and a black crow appeared on Ruby's bow. Startled, Gregor dropped the bow and shrieked. As Radkiel appeared once again, he picked up the bow and handed it to Ruby, whose mouth was hanging open. Raven started laughing at the younger teens because of the funny expressions on their faces. "What is so amusing this early in the morning?" yawned Adorna." Ruby pointed to Gregor, "He took my..."

"Please," Adorna smirked, "No shenanigans from you two, I missed two hours of beauty sleep to come train you little tyrants, so let's get on with it!" Just then, Serena came to the back of the shop with hot herbal tea and her infamous strawberry muffins. "No training, until you've all had some tea and muffins!" Her chestnut colored hair was piled loosely in a bun and her dark brown eyes sparkled when she smiled, "Oh Radkiel, I didn't know you were visiting, can I get you some of that special coffee you like?" Radkiel bowed, "No, thank you, Lady Serena, what you have here is plenty." He bowed again, and Serena blushed, "Okay then, good luck everyone!" Raven spoke up, as everyone grabbed a muffin and some tea, "Aunt Adorna, you didn't tell us we were also being trained by Mr.….." "It's Radkiel," smirked the Crop master.

"Yes, well," replied Adorna, "I was not sure he would be available, and luckily, he was. Now eat up, because we have a lot of work to do." Radkiel had been searching for an older wizard named Sagacity who had gone missing recently. The elder wizard was the oldest and wisest sorcerer in the kingdom.

Radkiel worked with Gregor and Ruby by honing their archery skills, while Adorna taught Raven fencing and sword fighting techniques. Raven was a quick study, and Adorna was relieved because she knew there was trouble brewing and the young one's talents would be needed when the time came to fight for Dragoness. She also knew, they had a long way to go, and frowned for a moment while lost in thought. "Take a break," Radkiel said to the students.

He walked over to Adorna, "Your thoughts, my lady?" "Adorna half smiled, "Ah, I'm showing my concern on my face again." "You are fearful?" asked the avian wizard. She brought her voice to a whisper as she looked to see where the teenagers were, "I dare not talk about it now, as I don't want to frighten them." "I sent them to get food," said Radkiel, "Please tell me what is troubling you." She looked at him, and he grabbed her hands. Adorna then told him, without going into detail, that they received a warning in the potions shop the other day, and why she thought Quagmire was trying to make a comeback. "He is going to try to destroy us all and take over the kingdom, I can feel it. I need to speak to the green goddess. She's the only one who can clear things up. If we could just be a step ahead of the dragon I'd feel better. There is so much we still don't know. Ever since that day, that horrible day….." A tear ran down her cheek. Radkiel put his arm around her protectively. "We will fight if we have to, and we will defeat Quagmire!" he hissed bitterly. "I feel like, I'm missing pieces of what happened that dreadful day, Radkiel, like my memory was erased. Don't you feel it? "Radkiel looked into Adorna's misty gray eyes, "I hate to admit it, but yes, I do feel fogginess about that fateful day, it's like a spell was cast over us, and it wiped out some memories of the event." Then at once they both said, "The Green Goddess!" Adorna grabbed Radkiel's hand, "I'm sure of it now, she's had to have had a hand in this somehow, but why? What was the good of making us forget the details, especially when we need to know everything to fight that wretched beast!" "She must have had her reasons," Radkiel said in a soothing tone. We can go to her together." He then lifted her right hand to his, and kissed it. "Adorna, my lady, there is something I have wanted to talk to you about…" "Oh shut up already!"

Raven yelled, as the young apprentice's came noisily back to the training room. Adorna snatched her hand away from Radkiel, but not soon enough for Ruby not to see. The girl turned slightly pink and said in a low voice, "I'm sorry, are we interrupting something?" "Hush," smiled Adorna, as she wagged her finger at Ruby, "You didn't see a thing."

When they were done training for the day, and completely exhausted, Radkiel said, "You all did wonderfully, and for a reward, you will have tomorrow off. After that, we will be here every day and there is no room for slacking. "Aunt Adorna, should we be worried," asked Ruby, sounding concerned. "We haven't really talked about the warning from that hideous vulture the other day, and now there's this rush to train all of a sudden…" Radkiel's eyebrows shot up, "Vulture, you were attacked? You didn't bother to tell me about that part!" Adorna patted his hand and looked at Ruby, "There is nothing for you to be concerned about as of yet. When I know more, I will let you know. For now, I need you to train, hone your skills, and be cautious. Anything out of the ordinary that happens, one of us elders needs to know, immediately. Gregor, please walk Ruby home, and tell lady Willow, I will speak to her later. Raven, please stay, I need to talk to you about something. Radkiel, can you come by Willow's later? "As you wish," he smiled, and bowed at the ladies as he left. Raven, I know you're only eighteen, but you are mature and wise beyond your years. With your mother's permission, I would like to take your sister on a mission with Radkiel and me. The reason I am telling you first before asking your mother is because I want to make sure both of your decisions are your own, and you are not influenced by Willow or anyone else about what I'm going to ask of you both."

Raven's eyes widened and Adorna realized she sounded ominous. She smiled, "I'm not trying to frighten you, and the particular task involving Ruby should not be too dangerous, but we still have to take every precaution because you never know. I'm going to tell you something now that you must keep to yourself. You cannot even tell Ruby because she doesn't have all of her powers yet, and she would be vulnerable. First, I need to ask you something. Have you fully come into your three highest powers? I know you have your telekinesis skill down, now what about the other two? I need to know this because I cannot give you training on those and need to find trainers skilled with those powers for you." Raven put her head down. Adorna gently lifted up her Goddaughter's chin, "No time to be ashamed, you've learned a lot in a short amount of time. You should be proud of yourself. It took me years of practice to sharpen my own skills. We all have different talents, now tell me." Raven began, "Yes, I'm completely comfortable with my telekinesis.

I have been using it for two years now, ever since I acquired it. I'm still having trouble with teleportation and spell casting." Adorna sighed, 'I know, it's too much all at once, plus your sword training. As you know, I can only advise you in sword training and telekinesis. I do know spells, and can cast, but it's not my power to teach. When you become an elder, so to speak, and trainer, The Green Goddess, Isoldina, grants you two powers that you may teach. Those wind up being your strongest talents. She does not grant more than two so that you become so attuned to your powers, you can use them with your eyes closed.

"I've heard of the green goddess," replied Raven, "But I thought she was just a fairy story I'd heard as a child." "She's more than just a fairy story," smiled Adorna, "And for what I'm about to tell you, I need you to be prepared. I need you to stay here to help guard dragoness, while we journey to see the goddess."

There was silence as everyone sat around the table at the Shadowstone home. It was a long night as they planned the trip to see the green goddess. One could not go empty handed, and gifts for the goddess had to be prepared and safely packed. Willow had called upon Phinnia, the Fairy queen to help with the preparations as she was the keeper of spells and enchantments. Daffilda, Phinnia's apprentice fairy, could transform herself to human size if need be, but she preferred her less obvious, normal dimension. As keeper of the spell book, known to the occupants of Dragoness as the 'Charmoire' she would also be training Raven in spell casting.

Phinnia had long dark hair, and beautiful sapphire blue wings that looked like delicate lace. She lived in the forest in a tree called the Spotted Elm, because of various big red dots on the woody trunk. The tree produced a magical sap used in healing potions. Also, it was a place where one could get a cocktail if he or she was of age. It looked more like a tavern than a magical tree, thus the illusion of a pub kept it safe from prying eyes. Tonight there would be a feast as all of the mystical creatures of the land gathered to help with Adorna's journey to see the green goddess. Stark Greywolf appeared just as everyone quieted down to eat. Ruby's eyes lit up as she saw her uncle enter the room. "Uncle Stark!" she yelled, as she ran over to hug him. Stark was Willow's younger brother. He was a wizard trainer, and the guardian of weaponry. Willow also ran over to her younger brother. "Well now brother, you are late, but just in time for dinner!" she quipped. Stark laughed a deep laugh and Raven giggled as she also greeted her uncle. As Serena walked by, to get a plate of food, Stark grabbed her hand and kissed it, "Lady Serena, you are as beautiful as ever." Startled by the compliment, and kiss, Serena blushed scarlet, and whispered,

"Thank you." and Stark laughed again. Stark then also took a plate of food and followed Serena to the long table of guests. Kerina, the Wicket queen was also there, while the other wickets were back in the forest guarding the land. Kerina had brought enchanted candles for Adorna to give to the goddess as her gift. She knew the goddess enjoyed the relaxing scent of vanilla and lilac, and made these candles especially for her. The candles exuded a calming aura, that lasted for days. As the rest of the guests arrived, the sky became overcast. Only two of the Feelers showed up, Callioth and Harmonia. The feelers were empaths, and though they were not as powerful as the goddess, they could sense things. Their intuition was stronger than the others in dragoness; they could feel danger. They also had the power of telekinesis, like Raven.

Sometimes they would have visions, but had to decipher the meanings, and they were great healers. The Feelers were always dressed in white and wore gold leaflet crowns on their heads; they were looked upon as doctors and holistic healers. They were well respected in the lands, and would travel as required to help those in need. Callioth explained that there was negative energy in the air so the other feelers stayed behind just in case of a crisis. Willow cleared her throat and said, "Dear friends of dragoness, I want to thank you all for coming. We've known for some time now that a shadow has fallen over our lands, and I'm sure we all want to know why." Everyone cheered as she continued, "Ever since, since," her voice cracked, and Stark came to his sister's side. She started again, "Excuse me, ever since Edrical, was killed by that monster, Quagmire," Phinnia spit at the sound of his name, then looked at Willow who nodded, "I have felt like I have been in a fog, I don't remember details, and it then Edrical was gone, and everything went back to normal the next day. I only remember bits and pieces. I can remember seeing my Edrical for the last time…" Stark caught his sister as she appeared faint. Callioth and Harmonia ran over and Harmonia said, "The poor woman is drained, she needs rest." Raven and Ruby ran to their mother's side, tears filling their eyes. Adorna clapped her hands, "Everyone please, quiet down." She looked at Willow who was trying to smile through her embarrassment. Willow nodded at Adorna to continue. "The girl's Godmother said, "This is a fact; we all vaguely remember what happened on that dreadful day. The girl's and I received a warning yesterday from a hideous creature, which we can assume came from the dark dragon's lair. If that was a warning, that means an attack is not far behind. We need to be prepared, but we also need answers so we know what to be prepared for. Radkiel, Ruby, and I will make the journey to see the green goddess. We will bring her all of your generous gifts, and hopefully, in return, she will help us see what we need to do to secure our land and defeat Quagmire, should he return. It will take us twenty-four hours to make the trip there and back as we have to go on foot to travel undetected. While we are gone, the rest of you must prepare your best powers of defense against dark sorcery, and protect all that is dear to us. "I will accompany you!" yelled out Stark. "No!" shouted Radkiel, "You are needed here!" "Do not tell me what I will or will not do, Radkiel," Stark shouted back, "You do not out rank me!" "Gentlemen please!" cried out Callioth, "Radkiel is right, Stark, I will send Thaddeus with them, it would be wise to have a healer with them." Willow spoke up, "They are right Stark, and I *do* need you here." "Stark softened his voice, "All right, but I'm warning you Radkiel, if anything happens to my niece…." and Stark stormed off. A piercing scream interrupted the festivities just as everyone was finishing their dessert. Flying into the house came Daffilda, Phinia's assistant fairy. "Oh gracious me," she wailed, as everyone looked on wearily. "What is it Daffilda?" questioned Phinia impatiently. "Oh I don't know where to begin," cried the befuddled fairy. Adorna stood up, "Dear Daffilda," she cooed in a soothing voice, take a deep breath, and tell us your news." This seemed to calm the anxious fairy and she continued, "I was flying around, looking for ingredients for an incantation. I was admiring all of the beautiful flowers that recently bloomed and wasn't paying attention to where I was going, terrible I know." Raven coughed and got a dirty look from her aunt. "Please continue," encouraged Adorna. "Oh yes," replied Daffilda, "I don't know how far I went or where it came from, but I was down on the ground, picking elderberries, when I saw something shiny." Daffilda's face turned three different shades of purple as she became anxious again. "Oh blasted, spit it out already!" squealed Phinnia. "I found…this!" Daffilda waved her hand and a considerably large egg appeared on the table. It was an odd light gray color with speckled red dots all over it. Everyone gasped as Adorna held up the egg, "Now we have another query for the green goddess," she said grimly, and everyone nodded in astonishment. "It could be one of the missing dragon's eggs," said Adorna, "It must be locked up with the trident for safe keeping!"

The green goddess, or Queen Isoldina, as she was commonly known, lived on Shimrock Mountain, in the Silver Forest. She was called the green goddess because of her holistic and natural ways of magic; she could also converse with animals. She was so beautiful; one would gasp at the sight of her. Her long blonde, almost white hair was long and wavy, and her piercing aqua eyes always had a worried look in them. Right now she was pacing the floor, the train of her sparkling emerald green dress trailing behind her. "She closed her eyes for a moment, "I can sense evil, Ambrosia," she said to her loving, colorful parrot. Ambrosia nodded and squawked, "Evil!" "We will have visitors soon, and I'm not sure if I'm ready for them," the goddess went on, "If only Edrical…." she bit her lip, and then shook her head, "Never mind, I must stop thinking of the past," she said sadly. "Forget the past!" Ambrosia agreed. Isoldina smiled as she pet the bird's head, "We have to do what we can to help, and so we will wait for our old friends to arrive."

Getting there was not going to be an easy task. The group would have to first make a portal at the end of the woods of Dragoness. "Ruby, do you have everything you need?" asked Adorna? "I think so, Aunt Adorna," she replied nervously. "The only thing we need is a vile of sap from The Dotted Elm." "You are not going there alone." said Radkiel sternly. The Dotted Elm was about a mile from the potions shop, and was actually constructed inside the enormous, odd looking tree. Sometimes, the younger ones tried to sneak in and get a peek at the bar, but Crizal, the barkeep was always there to make sure there were no shenanigans going on. Ruby frowned, "I'm not a baby, you know!" Her eye started to twitch. "Ah, ah, ah!" scolded Adorna, "We will not have any arguments, and I wasn't going to send her alone, Radkiel." Ruby rolled her eyes. Radkiel smirked. Just then Thaddeus appeared and said, "I am ready for our journey." "Thaddeus," replied Adorna, "Would you be as kind as to accompany Ruby to The Dotted Elm? Crizal, the proprietor will be there waiting for you with a vial. Please be careful, and do not dawdle. Radkiel and I will wait for you at the end of the forest. We need the vial for the spell to open the portal. She only had enough time to make the one vial so you must be cautious with it." Thaddeus bowed, "On my honor, my lady, we will be most cautious."

Adorna smiled, "Thank you." then she hugged Ruby, and squeezed Thaddeus' shoulder. "If you both have your packs ready, then there's no time to waste, Radkiel and I will see you shortly, remember, Kerina, the wicket queen will be waiting for you at the back of the potions shop, she will guide you to the end of the forest, Radkiel and I have a few more things to do here."

When Ruby and Thaddeus set off, Radkiel whispered to Adorna, "I'm very concerned." Adorna put her fingers to her lips, "Shhh!" and motioned for him to follow her outside. "I don't want Willow to hear you; she's been under enough stress." "I'm sorry," grimaced Radkiel, "I don't understand why we are taking Ruby with us when Raven has her full powers already." Adorna smirked, "This is exactly why," answered the swordswoman, "I need Raven here with Stark to protect her mother, and the trident. Ruby, although she doesn't know it yet, is an empath."

Radkiel's eyes widened. Adorna continued, we may need

her skill on our journey." Radkiel sputtered, "How, how can she be an empath when she shoots fire from her eyes uncontrollably when she gets angry?" He looked at Adorna, bewildered. She laughed, "Ah, you don't know much about witches' powers, nor women, do you?" Radkiel's face turned pink as Adorna chuckled again. "She is much better at controlling her fire power, and we will have Thaddeus, who is also an empath, and a healer with us. Besides, she went on; during breaks you can teach her your avian skills." Radkiel's mouth dropped open. Adorna chuckled once more, "Yes, she inherited wizardry from her father, and this is her destiny. Now open the door and close your mouth before a tweedle bug flies in it, there's no time to tend to wounds. Radkiel picked up his bag and held the door open for Adorna. They assured Willow they would be safe and look after Ruby. After Raven hugged her aunt and Radkiel, the swordswoman, and wizard headed to the potions shop to pick up last minute supplies.

Serena heard the door jingle and looked up from the new spell she was reading. She smiled when she saw Adorna and Radkiel. Then she turned serious. "Are you sure you need to take this trip?" she asked, sounding concerned. Radkiel looked at Adorna who smiled grimly, "Serena, I know you're worried, but I can feel Quagmire, I can feel his wrath, his pain. He is bent on revenge. I fear if we don't seek the help of Queen Isoldina, we will get blindsided. We need her help." Serena glanced at Radkiel, and in a gentle voice said, "Does Ruby know about…" Adorna gave her a warning glance and shook her head. Radkiel raised his eyebrows, "What is it I don't know!" Adorna sighed, as Serena mouthed 'sorry.' "I'll tell you later Radkiel; we have to go, now!" Serena gave her a velvet pouch with an elixir in it, and off they went. "Safe journey!" Serena yelled, as her friends rushed through the back door. Ruby, Thaddeus, and Kerina were waiting for Adorna and Radkiel at the edge of the lake near the end of the forest. "Did you have any problems at The Dotted Elm?" queried Radkiel. Ruby smirked, and Thaddeus's face turned bright red. "No problems," giggled Ruby, "But I think Crizal has a crush on Thaddeus!" Thaddeus looked down at his feet, and Radkiel laughed out loud. Adorna cleared her throat, "Yes, well, Thaddeus can worry about that later, we have a journey to begin, but first we must open the portal. I need the sap from the dotted elm. Ruby handed her aunt the vial of sap, and Adorna mixed it with the elixir Serena gave her. She then threw the mixture into the lake. "Make sure you hold onto your belongings, grab hands, and repeat after me!" Kerina bid them farewell, but waited to make sure the portal opened before she left. Adorna chanted, "A journey to the goddess, we seek thine help, open the portal, we bring you wealth, as loyal subjects of Equonicous, we plead you Queen Isoldina, we are in distress!" Suddenly a mist appeared, and a big gust of wind, as the travelers tightly gripped each other's hands and their belongings. It became quiet, as a big circle opened in the lake where Adorna threw the potion. Kerina yelled, "Safe Journey, don't dawdle, it won't stay open long!" Ruby looked at her aunt nervously; she wasn't fond of the water. Then Adorna smiled at her, and Ruby could hear her aunt's voice in her head, *"It's okay, we are going to jump down together, we will not be submerged in water, trust me."* Ruby nodded, and Adorna yelled, "Everyone ready, at the count of three, one two, three!"

"Oof!" cried out Radkiel. "That was a rough landing." Ruby's breath came out in a whoosh, "Whew, I'm glad that part is over with." "For now," replied Radkiel, we have to do it again to get home." Adorna and Thaddeus both gave him a dirty look, as Ruby's mouth opened. "Wow, what is this place!" asked Ruby in awe of her surroundings. "It may look pretty," said Thaddeus, "But be careful, there are creatures here that are protective of their land, and will not appreciate trespassers. Don't forget, they were run out of Ralliant when the Murk brothers took over the land." "But we are good," surmised Ruby, "We mean them no harm." "Yes, continued Thaddeus, but they may not know that at first." Ruby was amazed at what she saw, sure Dragoness was beautiful, but this place was ethereal, it sparkled, glistened even.

Everything from the trees to the flowers appeared to be silver, and glinted in the sunlight. "Are those roses?" asked Ruby. "Yes," replied Adorna, and they are very sacred to the queen, she err... she planted them herself years back and…." "Radkiel threw up his hand, "Quiet!" he hissed. There's someone else here!"

Back in dragoness, Stark was pacing the floor at Willow's house. Willow placed her hand gently on his shoulder, "Stark please eat something," she frowned, "Starving yourself with worry is not going to get them home any faster." "I'm not hungry!" he groused. "I'm uneasy about his Radkiel fellow." Willow looked at her brother questioningly, then it dawned on her, and she smirked, "Ah ha, you're in love with Adorna, and you're jealous!" For a moment, Stark turned pale, and then he exclaimed, "That's not it at all, I'm worried about Ruby." The truth was, he'd always held a torch for the green goddess, but never felt worthy of her. "Mmhmm," teased Willow. "Sister, I swear…" he started, but was interrupted when Raven ran into the room, breathless, "Quick, help," She took a deep gulp of air, "What is it?" exclaimed Willow as Stark ran over to his niece who had a bruise on her cheek and was bleeding. "At the Shop, Serena," and then Raven fainted. "Stay with her!" Stark shouted as he ran out the door. When he got to the shop, Stark noticed it was dark inside. He stepped cautiously as he opened the door. It looked like a warzone. Glass was smashed everywhere, the floor was slippery, and pages were torn from books. He could hear weeping coming from the back room. "Who's there!" he yelled. Phinnia and Daffilda appeared, one of Phinnia's wings looked damaged, and she had dirt smudged on her face. Daffilda was hysterical and Stark couldn't make out what she was trying to tell him. He didn't want to do it, but he had to snap her out of it, "Daffilda!" he roared. She immediately stopped crying, and looked at him in shock. "I'm sorry," he said in a lighter tone, "I need you to calm down, and tell me what went on here, so I can help." Phinnia wearily sat on a bench, and winced. "OH oh, yes, "I'm sorry master Stark!" Gently, as to not frighten her again he said, "Please tell me what happened." "Lady Serena, she was taken!" sniffed the apprentice fairy. "Taken!" exclaimed Stark, "By whom?" "That's just it sir, we are not sure, it was an awful creature!" her voice rose again. Seeing Phinnia wanted to speak, and knowing she was the more level-headed of the two, Stark said, "Daffilda, I need you to go find Callioth and Harmonia. Tell them what happened and that Phinnia needs her wing mended. Also, send word to the wicket queen, Kerina, we will need all the help we can get. "Oh yes, my lord," agreed Daffilda, and she left. Phinia sat up straighter, and Stark helped her, "Can you talk?" She shook her head, and then started, "We were having tea, and Lady Serena was conjuring up some new spells, spells to ward off dark magic. Raven was helping her, and using her telekinesis, and practicing her power by moving things to Serena's cauldron. Raven was just about to add the last ingredient to the mixture, when all of a sudden there was a loud rumbling.

Things started falling off the shelves, and crashing to the floor. Phinnia's eyes widened, then it appeared, a dark creature, it looked like a wolfen, but it had wings, big wings. Raven tried moving daggers at it, but it was too quick, and when Lady Serena went to cast a spell, it swooped her up and took her away, just flew out the door and disappeared, it was dreadful!"

The exhausted fairy sagged down in the chair. Stark patted her tiny hand, and said kindly, "It wasn't your fault," but inside he was seething, "*I have to find Serena, and protect this land until the others get back!*"

"What is that noise?" whispered Adorna, sounding guarded. Everyone stood quietly, waiting. Abruptly, Radkiel whirled around in the direction of the noise. He put his fingers to his lips, signaling everyone to be quiet, he then pointed to an oddly shaped bush with pointed leaves. It appeared the bush was moving. "All right!" shouted Radkiel, "Show yourself, or face the consequences!" Everyone moved into attack stance as they waited for whoever was hiding in the bush to come out. Then, someone quietly stepped out with his hands out in front of him and Ruby squealed, "Gregor!" "Gregor!" the adults repeated in astonishment. "What are you doing here?" asked Radkiel in an annoyed tone. Gregor looked around sheepishly and said, "Okay, don't get angry, I just wanted to help. I…I was worried about Ruby." Thaddeus smirked, and Radkiel smacked his forehead with his hand. Adorna started to smile, but then said in a stern voice, "Gregor, although your intentions are admirable, I hope you realize that we have serious business to take care of here. There will be no shenanigans, or pranks. Do you understand?" Gregor nodded as he glanced at Ruby, who was blushing and looking all around.

"How did you get here?" asked Thaddeus. Gregor smiled broadly, "Oh that was easy, I shrunk myself down and hid in Radkiel's satchel." Radkiel's mouth dropped open, and the rest of the group started laughing. A loud screech from above had the merriment come to an abrupt stop. Ruby put her fingers in her ears to drown out the sound. Thaddeus closed his eyes for a moment and then re-opened them. "This is not good," he said aloud, "It's a warning, and I'm getting a feeling that something…..something." He looked at Adorna who shook her head.

"Ruby, Gregor, I need both of you to see how many can-

dles we have, I know Kerina was given some by the wickets."
Then Adorna took Thaddeus and Radkiel aside. "Okay,"
whispered Adorna, "What did you see Thaddeus?" "It's not
so much a seeing, my lady; it's more of a feeling. Something
happened back at dragoness and I sense danger there. We
need to get on with this journey before anything else
happens." Radkiel looked grim as he said, "Okay everyone
we need to start moving toward Shimrock Mountain. Do
not touch anything, only Thaddeus and Adorna will know
what is safe." As the group started to move, Adorna said to
Ruby, "There is something I must tell you before we get to
the queen, and it's going to be a surprise to you, but it's
something you must know. Ruby's eyes widened. Adorna
patted her hand then said, "We will have to camp out at the
bottom of the mountain tonight, we should be safe. I'm sure
the goddess knows we are on our way, as she opened the
portal. We should look for a place to camp and then we will
eat. While we are eating, I have something I have to explain,
before we meet with the queen goddess." Radkiel quickly
brushed his hand over Adorna's and she gave him a warm
smile. "My lady," he whispered, "There is something I
would like to speak to you about also." Adorna looked away
coyly as she nodded, and they all headed toward the mountain to look for a place to camp.

Serena tried to open her eyes, but they felt very heavy. She grabbed for her neck, and felt around, her amulet was still there, not that it did her much good before she was taken, but the secret latch in the back of it hadn't opened, so she still had some magic in it. She felt around with her hands. It felt like she was on a dirt floor. He feet were bound, but her hands were free, which she thought was odd. Then she realized why she couldn't see, her eyes were covered.

She tried to take the covering off of her eyes, but she was weak, and her arm fell back at her side. She tried to sit up, and felt dizzy. Then she smelled an awful odor, almost like sulfur and she wrinkled her nose, trying not to gag at the stench. A hairy hand brushed across her face and she cringed. "Who are you!" she demanded. A deep voice laughed, it was almost like a growl, "I am a sycophant, a servant of Quagmire." "Quagmire?" questioned Serena, "Then he's… he's…." "Yesss," hissed the creature, he is alive, weak, but alive. He will rule Equonicous once everything is in place and he has the trident." Serena tried again to sit up, "He will never get the trident, nor will he ever rule Equonicous!" She fell back weak from her effort. "Rest up my dear," said the foul smelling beast, you'll need your strength!" She was alone again, and tried to summon up some energy to get up, but whatever she was given was very strong and she fell back yet again. She wanted to cry, but fell into a deep sleep instead, dreaming of dragoness and wicked creatures.

Willow, Stark and Raven were back at the potions shop. When they got there Willow looked at Stark, astonished at the destruction she saw. The trio heard noises coming from the back room, and Stark held the women back as he crept stealthily ahead of them. Then he said to Willow and Raven, "It's okay, c'mon back." There, on the couch in the training room lay Phinnia with Callioth hunched over her, reciting a healing incantation. Daffilda looked on concernedly, and Kerina tried tidying up. Harmonia looked at the newcomers and said in a grim tone, "The good news is, Phinnia's wing should be healed in twenty-four hours, and the bad news is we still haven't figured out who or what took Serena. I tried my divining pendulum to locate her whereabouts, but the stone keeps turning black." Raven gasped loudly, "You don't think she's, she's…." "No," Harmonia replied gently, I would have felt that." It's more likely that she is incapacitated at the moment, either asleep or unconscious." Willow frowned, "Kerina isn't there anything you could do?" she asked the wicket queen. "Kerina replied gruffly, "These things take time, I have some of my people at the Dotted Elm, collecting sap to make a liquid seeing, but they have to be careful, there are probably spies about!" Stark nodded as Raven asked, "Excuse me, what is a liquid seeing?" Kerina grunted as she went about cleaning up broken glass, and muttered under her breath about younglings. Harmonia answered, "A liquid seeing is when we add the ingredients to the seeing spell into a cauldron to make a casting, and then we can see, in the liquid, what we ask to see. Since we are low on supplies right now because of all the destruction to the store, we need to harvest more ingredients, which Queen Kerina has so graciously asked her trollions to acquire." Knowing how Kerina felt about non-trollions at times, Stark bowed and said, "Thank you Queen Kerina, your help is much appreciated." Willow and Raven did the same, and the grumpy wicket queen, grinned and said, "Yes, yes, enough of that drivel, you're welcome." Harmonia stifled a giggle. Kerina could be rough at times, but she did have a big heart, and cared about all the people and creatures of the land. She just didn't have any patience and was easily annoyed. "Since there is nothing we can do until we receive the supplies we need, you may as well help with the clean up." Kerina motioned to Stark, Willow and Raven. Raven opened her mouth to say something, but Willow gave her a warning glance.

"Her majesty is right," said Willow, "We must all work together." Willow handed Stark a broom, and while Callioth continued to treat Phinnia, the rest of the group got to work restoring the shop as best they could, all of them anxious with their own thoughts of what lie ahead.

Settling near an empty cave, Adorna, Ruby, Thaddeus

and Gregor, all sat down on the gravel wearily. A fire was started and everyone ate a meal of bread, cheese, and fruit. Ruby took a swig of water from her canteen and said, "Okay aunt Adorna, what are you keeping from me?"

Adorna took a deep breath and said, "I need all of you to hear this, not just Ruby. It will make some things a little clearer, but most of all to Ruby." Everyone waited for Adorna to begin as dusk began to fall. "A long time ago," began Adorna, "When I was a young girl first learning my powers, I met your father Edrical, Ruby, when my parents and I fled to Dragoness from the land that is now known as, 'The Island of Murk.' There were two dark wizards at the time, who called themselves the 'Mirthless Murk's,' they were twin brothers. Their parents, one of whom was an evil warlock, and the other a dark witch, raised the brothers to do their bidding. They wanted to take over the four kingdoms of Equonicous which included Dragoness, Silver Mountain, which is where we are now, Beauteous, where King Edgeworth and Queen Primrose reign, and Wickardia, which is where our friends the wickets are from. Ruby, and Gregor, you two are only familiar with Dragoness, and will soon be familiar with Silver Mountain. Unfortunately, from what I've heard, Murk Island, named for its new inhabitants, once the brothers took over, is still shadowed in darkness. The Murk brother's parents were killed when they got into a battle with the dragon mother, Eragonia. We elders along with Eragonia were protectors of dragoness. The dragons in our land were almost extinct except for Eragonia and her eggs. Dracha and Xenos Murk, the brother's parents, wanted to take over Equonicous. Once the twin's parents were killed, the dark land became home to Quagmire, the dark dragon, and could still be, no one knows for certain. Ruby's eyes widened and she went to grab Gregor's hand, but quickly dropped it and blushed. The elder's pretended they didn't notice. Gregor asked, "What happened to Eragonia?" Radkiel took a deep breath, "Unfortunately, she was killed in the battle with the elder Murk's, but not before leaving her eggs to be hidden in Dragoness for protection. All three were supposed to be hidden separately until it was safe for them to be hatched, but somehow, one of the twins stole one of the eggs and through some dark sorcery, was able to hatch it. In doing so, the hatchling, whom we now call Quagmire, was born and raised by the Murk brothers for their own evil agenda, convincing the dragon that the entire kingdom was against him. Adorna nodded gravely, and continued, "The Murk's powers became stronger as the years went by. Before their deaths, Dracha and Xenos sought out every diabolical witch, warlock, goblin, urchin, and creature they could find to teach the brothers all elements of the dark arts. They practiced daily and became stronger and wicked as the days went by, but, they are both irresponsible and unintelligent. Before the land became the Island of Murk, it was a lovely oasis. It was called the land of Ralliant, named as a place that anyone could go to, to live in harmony, enjoy the splendor of the land, and rally together. There was a glistening waterfall, where beautiful Chimera fish used to swim, happily amongst the mer-people. The water had healing powers and once a year, during the 'Fair of Ralliant,' anyone who was pure of heart, could take a dip in the water, and any ailment that was bestowed on them, would be healed. For example, if a warrior from the kingdom received an injury, her or she, whatever the injury would be healed in the mystical water."

Thaddeus smiled as he touched a spot on his lower left arm, "I remember like it was yesterday," he whispered, "I was just a young soldier, and got seared by an enemies' sword. It was a verge assailant, and I was caught off guard. I was assigned to protect the queen's ladies, and a verge somehow invaded the castle. Horrible creatures they were, I shudder at the thought! Luckily, before anymore invaders could get in, the other soldiers were alerted and the one invader was captured. The rest is a little foggy to me now, but I remember being told while I was recovering from the attack, that I could go to Ralliant that summer to get healed, and I did. I will never forget how beautiful the waterfall was…" Thaddeus' voice trailed off sadly. Adorna noticed Ruby and Gregor's eyes were getting heavy, and she clapped her hands together. The two teens sat up straighter, startled by the sudden burst of sound. "I know you two are exhausted," Adorna started, "But I need you to stay awake a little while longer. It's important I tell you everything, so you are prepared before we move forward with our journey tomorrow.

Adorna cleared her throat, quickly glanced at Radkiel, and then focused on Ruby. "What?" asked Ruby. "Why is everyone looking at me like that?" Adorna smiled, "Ruby, when Radkiel, Thaddeus, the other elders, and I were around yours and Gregor's age, King Edgeworth was just forming his army of knights, or warriors, as we now call them. At that time the goddess Isoldina, who is also queen Primrose' sister fell in love with one of the soldiers. That soldier was your father, Edrical." "Whoa," said Gregor. Radkiel glared at him. Ruby took in a sharp breath, "Go on," she whispered. Adorna went on, "This was also when the people from Ralliant were fleeing from the island. A lot of occupants of Ralliant died trying to escape. Everything was happening all at once and King Edgeworth was trying to put together an army to defeat the Murk brothers. As the days went on, and the brother's powers became stronger, the island of Ralliant became darker, and murkier, until everything that was beautiful dried up and died.

Ruby wiped a tear from her eye, as did Thaddeus, while Gregor tried to hide his face, not wanting anyone to see his emotions. Radkiel gently placed his hand on Adorna's, "Let me finish the story, my lady, your voice is getting hoarse." The swordswoman smiled, "Thank you, I am getting a bit tired." "Isoldina," Radkiel explained, was about your age Ruby, at that time, maybe a year or two older. She served as her sister's lady in waiting, but also was developing her powers. I'm not sure if you and Gregor know this, but, neither a king nor queen can attain or use magical powers. It would be against the law of our lands. "Why is that?" asked Gregor, sounding confused. "Because, they are rulers, and it would give them an unfair advantage to have that kind of power. It was written in the scrolls long ago. "What if they were born with powers, and can't help it?" wondered Ruby. "Then their powers had to be stripped from them if they wanted to rule," explained Thaddeus, "They are given a choice to either become a ruler, if they are born into the role, or keep their powers, study, and become whomever they chose."

"Wow!" Ruby and Gregor replied in unison. "I don't understand," began Ruby, "How can Isoldina rule over Silver Mountain, if she has magical powers?" Adorna cleared her throat again, and squeezed Radkiel's shoulder, "When Isoldina was at court, tending to her sister, and studying with her tutors, she had met Edrical outside one day. He had been watching her during archery practice. She became very good archer. She was just finishing up a task of hitting an apple from the orchard tree, when Edrical unfortunately stepped under the tree and got hit on the head with the apple, after he ducked from the arrow. At first, Isoldina was annoyed that he got in the way of her arrow, firstly because he could have been hurt, and secondly because she thought it reflected badly on her skill. But then, just as she was going to tear into Edrical, he blurted out, "*Why thank you my lady, I did so need a snack*," and he bowed. She started laughing, and then he started laughing, and they became inseparable, every day after for months. Now don't forget, Adorna continued, everyone from Ralliant who had escaped, came to either Beauteous, or Shimrock Mountain and became a courtier, or a soldier if they stayed at the castle. Some fled to the Mountain to make homes, and received help from the king and queen, but everyone lived in fear. If the Murk brothers could take over and destroy Ralliant, they were capable of anything. It just was not clear how they were becoming so powerful. The king surmised that the twins must have been getting help, but no one could figure out from whom. Then it happened, one day the king and queen received word from a feeler named Hannart that the Murk brothers came across a dragon's egg. Back then, despite what is thought now, dragons were born gentle creatures, even with their mystical powers. It was how they were brought up and trained that determined their outcome, so to speak. Before the Murk brothers were born, we were on good terms with the dragon mother. Unfortunately, one of the eggs was stolen from Dragoness." "Dragoness!" exclaimed Ruby and Gregor in unison again.

Radkiel smiled, "That is where the name of our land comes from. "The brother's only stole one egg?" asked Gregor. "One egg was all they could find," replied Radkiel, before the brothers were found out." Ruby groused, as she yawned, "What does this have to do with my father and the goddess?" "Bear with us, dear," replied Adorna, "We are trying to get in every detail, sorry for the back and forth. After, Eragonia laid the eggs; they were hidden, each with a guardian, until it was time for the baby dragons to be born, safely. It was considered if the eggs were spread out and hidden, instead of all together, the babies would be less vulnerable. When the one egg was stolen, we knew before long there would be a battle to contend with. As the Murk brothers were fleeing with the egg, one of our friends, a wizard named Sagacity, had almost caught up with the evil worms when suddenly, Nefari turned around and cast a spell, which ricochet off a stone, and knocked Sagacity out. The last thing he remembered was the brothers escaping through a portal, and hearing the second brother Querd say,

"We are on our way brother to rule the kingdom!" Then Sagacity blacked out. Radkiel took it from there, "The king decided to send his army, which included Edrical to find Murk Island, and destroy the brothers before they could do anymore harm. He felt the army was strong enough now, and the wizards, witches, and all the magical folks of the kingdom would be strong enough to take the brother's on. Since the elder Murks had passed on; it was thought that the brothers would be vulnerable. Isoldina went to the king and queen and begged them to let her and Edrical marry first before they sent him off to fight, because he had proposed to her a week earlier, but they denied the request because they didn't want any distractions, and they felt the army should head right off. Isoldina was extremely upset at their decision and went into a depression. She refused to leave the castle tower, and hardly ate. No matter what the king or queen did to try to please her or take her mind off of Edrical, she would not budge, until one day she received a letter from her fiancé saying how he missed her, and how grim his and the other soldier's journey had been. They wrote to each other frequently, and Isoldina began to come out of her depression, and took up her studies once more. Whenever she felt down, she tried to think about her beloved's return, and their future plans. Her powers became stronger, and the king and queen felt safer in the knowledge they had someone powerful with them at the castle. You see, as long as the rulers had their magical courtiers use their powers for good, they could have them as allies. If they felt threatened, as in the case with the Murks, they could send their guards, whether they had powers or not to protect the lands and kingdom, and that was and is still the rule. Those who lacked in magical powers were twice as strong in their defensive prowess. Gregor and Ruby both yawned again. Adorna smiled, "Just a little longer, I promise. Thaddeus!" Thaddeus sat up and looked sheepish, "So sorry, must have nodded off." Radkiel snickered. "This is where it gets more difficult," sighed Adorna. All of a sudden, the letters stopped. Months went by and no one had heard from the king's army. The king sent out more soldiers to look for the first group, but to no avail, it was like they vanished." Ruby's eyes grew larger. Adorna went on, "Sorrowful, and disappointed with the bleak news, the king and queen signed off that their first army as dead. Isoldina went into a rage and refused to talk to anyone or continue with her studies. At this time, the king and queen decided to give Isoldina Shimrock Mountain, to watch over. This would provide a distraction for her and some relief for the rulers as many people who fled Ralliant had set up homes in Shimrock Mountain, and needed protection. She was allowed to take any guards with her of her choosing, but she chose to go alone, telling her sister and the king that she would train her own army. They even sent Isoldina a beautiful rare parrot, which the goddess named Ambrosia, to keep her company. All ruling decisions though still had to go through the king and queen as per the law, but Isoldina could pretty much reign as she see fit."

Adorna started coughing and took a drink of water. "Allow me," Thaddeus said, "It will help keep me awake." What happened to my father? Blurted Ruby, was he hurt?" Gregor sat up taller. "He was not hurt," replied Thaddeus, "The army would make a different camp every few days, in case the enemy was close by. They wanted to be a step ahead of the game. Your father was the captain of the army, but he did not have his full powers yet. Being Sagacity had fully recovered from his attack by the Murk brothers, the king had allowed him to go with the soldiers. It was always good to have a wizard and a feeler with the army or at least one or the other. One day, when they found a hidden cave, which they thought might be a gateway to The Island of Murk, the army all ascended into the cave. Suddenly, as half of the soldiers got into the cave, there was an intense clap of thunder. There before them appeared a diabolical sorceress by the name of Iniquitous. She was thought to have been the Murk brother's aunt, and became guardian of the baby dragon, whom they named, "Quagmire!" Ruby and Gregor both shouted at once. This time it was Radkiel who was startled after nodding off. At hearing the name, 'Quagmire,' he jumped up, and drew his sword. The others laughed for a moment, and Radkiel rolled his eyes, and sat back down. "Now that I have everyone's attention, I'll continue," smirked Thaddeus. After Iniquitous appeared, the army tried to retreat from the cave, but the evil witch cast her wand toward the ground, and the ground began to split in half. The army would have been swallowed up except Iniquitous didn't realize there was a wizard amongst the soldiers. Sagacity was disguised in soldier's armor, not his usual wizard robes.

Quickly, he threw off his helmet, and cast his wand toward the dark witch, temporarily knocking her down. Her wand fell, and Sagacity was able to whisk the army to Dragoness through a portal he rapidly devised by using what he had left of a potion he brought with him that contained sap from the dotted elm. When they landed in Dragoness, the soldiers were very weary. Some were injured from the journey, having to fight small battles along the way with various creatures the brothers had placed their way. Sagacity looked upon various homes to shelter the warriors until they could make their way back to Beauteous. A lot of time had passed from when they started the journey to find The Island of Murk. The brother's with the help of Iniquitous had cast several protective charms around the Island to shield it from intruders, making it practically impenetrable. Thaddeus looked at Ruby, and cleared his throat, "Your mother was in Serena's potions shop one day, purchasing ingredients for a healing potion, when your father walked into the shop. He had heard of the healing herbs and salves that were sold at the shop and was inquiring about them to Serena as your mother walked in from the back room. Edrical locked eyes with her and they both smiled. When Willow found out Edrical was a royal soldier, and of the army's plight, she asked him if he and the men had a place to stay until their journey back to the castle. He said they were going to stay at a farmer's barnyard. Willow would not hear of it and she offered them to stay at the cottage on your grandparent's property, which now is your mother's, as you already know. When your mother inherited the cottage after your grandparents had passed on, she always kept it in order in honor of them. Edrical accepted the kind offer and Sagacity was happy to know the warriors would get a good rest. Sagacity also felt it was time to educate Edrical on his wizard studies, and he began his lessons at the potions shop a week later. Edrical, not remembering much about Isoldina because he had thought she had forgotten him, fell deeply in love with Willow. When he stopped receiving letters from Isoldina, he felt ignored and tried to put his heartbreak in the back of his mind. Neither Isoldina nor Edrical had realized at the time that their letters were intercepted by a minion of Iniquitous. She figured that if the goddess and the captains of the king's army were both suffering from heart ache, they would both be vulnerable, not having their wits about them." "Aunty," Ruby spoke up, "I really need to sleep, I think we all do." "I know Red, we are all exhausted, but, try to hold on a little longer, I promise I'm almost finished, and I'll even let you sleep a little later in the morning than we intended." "Okay, "Ruby and Gregor both agreed warily. "I'll try to shorten up the rest," replied Adorna. Gregor snorted, "Now she says that." Radkiel gave him a dirty look, and Adorna continued, "Okay, in a nutshell, Willow and Edrical married. Once the warriors were well rested and strong again, Edrical sent them back to the castle with a note for the king and queen explaining his marriage to Willow and how he would now reside with her in Dragoness. Sagacity officiated the wedding of Willow and Edrical in the forest behind the potions shop. It was a beautiful ceremony, and all of the magical creatures were in attendance. "Ahem," Coughed Radkiel. Adorna laughed, "Oops, sorry, I forgot, no more details! Anyway, the king and queen were very fond of Edrical, so they were not upset with his decision to marry Willow. Her parents were great courtiers to them at one time, and deeply respected in Dragoness. What they feared was Isoldina's reaction when she found out, so they didn't tell her. A few years went by, and Raven was born. Everything seemed to be fine in the kingdom. Another few years later, you were born, Ruby. Again, everything seemed quiet and everyone went about their daily business until one day, while Edrical was outside with Raven, teaching her some wizardly tricks he learned from Sagacity, darkness appeared over the sun. The whole land became cloaked in darkness. Then everything started shaking like an earth quake. Edrical grabbed Raven and ran inside. He and Willow took Ruby and Raven to the potions shop. I happened to be there at the time training some of the young wizards in sword fighting, in the training room. I had already been at the front of the shop when Willow and Edrical came in with you children. We hid you and your sister at The Spotted Elm with the fairies, and then came back to Serena's. We all went outside, and Serena screamed and pointed to the sky. Flying down was Iniquitous on a now full grown Quagmire. He was breathing fire, and we could feel the heat as they came closer. Abruptly, one of the young wizards whom I was just training cried out in searing pain, as one of the Murk brothers, Querd, struck him with a blow from his wand. I whipped around and clipped him with my dagger which infuriated Iniquitous. An immense fight ensued and just as we thought we were going to defeat the invaders, Iniquitous pulled out her wand. Surprised at this turn of events, Edrical was not prepared when Iniquitous blocked his wand cast, and zapped back at him with her intricate wand. None of us had seen anything like it before. Edrical tried to conjure his trident, but the missing onyx that belonged in the handle of the trident rendered it powerless against the sorceress' black magic. Thaddeus tried to intervene but was knocked unconscious. After he was weakened by Iniquitous' bolt, Edrical bravely trying to protect us, threw Willow to the ground, and leapt up at Quagmire hoping to gouge his throat with his sword. His wizarding powers were weak, and he didn't count on the strength of the wicked dragon. That's when Quagmire struck him down." Ruby put her head into Gregor's shoulder, and he held her. "I'm so, so sorry Ruby," Adorna whispered. "Why, why are you telling us all of this!" the girl shouted. Adorna choked on a sob, and Radkiel put his arm around her. Thaddeus spoke up, "Because, you need to know that this is why we have to make this journey. Our purpose is to trek up this mountain to ask for the goddess' help. When your father died, Isoldina felt it; she felt a searing pain go through her body. When she found out your father had been betrothed to your mother, and then he was killed by Quagmire, she vowed to never come down from the mountain, and that she would never love another. She also claimed she would never forgive any of us for what happened. She still hasn't, after all these years, spoken to the king or queen. "Then why should we seek her help? Why should we have to grovel if she hates us so much?" Adorna replied softly, "Because there is evidence that

Quagmire is still alive. When your father was killed, your mother went into a rage. With the help of the feelers, she was able to vanquish Iniquitous, and hide the trident, but, Quagmire and the brother's are still out there somewhere waiting for the right time to attack us again, and we need Isoldina's help. She had placed a sleeping spell on the land after the attack because it was so devastating to our people, and she didn't want them to remember the ugliness of the battle. Even though she was angry, she has a good heart, even if it *was* broken. "How come you all remember what happened?" asked Gregor. "Because we were the ones in the battle, replied Thaddeus, and maybe because she wanted us to remember the pain." Radkiel's eyes searched Adorna's, "If only I had gotten there in time…" his voice cracked. "Shhh," Adorna soothed, "You couldn't have known, you were at a training retreat, now is not the time for blame." "It's time we get some sleep," said Thaddeus. "I don't think I'll get any sleep now, after hearing all of this." declared Ruby. "Neither will I," stated Gregor.

Thaddeus winked at Adorna and Radkiel as he secretly pointed his wand at the youngsters and murmured, "Slumberous." Ruby and Gregor fell fast asleep, as the elders made plans for the adventure ahead.

"Shhhh, try not to move yet." a voice whispered. Serena tried to sit up anyway, startled, as she groggily awoke. "Who…are…you?" she rasped in a hoarse voice. She was so thirsty, and her throat hurt. She felt a hand touch the side of her head and she shrunk back. "It's okay," the voice continued to whisper, "I'm not going to hurt you. Give me a minute to get this blindfold off of you." Serena stayed still as she felt the blindfold being gently cut off. It took a few moments for her eyes to focus, and then she saw a man looking at her concernedly. He had kind eyes, but looked troubled and he seemed pained. She could tell under normal circumstances he was probably a very handsome man, but looked haggard and weak now. "Thank you sir," Serena whispered gratefully. "Here," he said kindly, "Drink this." Serena looked at him. "I promise you it's just water," he said soothingly. Serena tried to smile and let him help her take a sip of water from the metal pitcher. He handed Serena a small knife, and she unbound her legs. Then she noticed the man's right arm, and how it hung limp to his side. "Oh!" she exclaimed, as she went over to him, "You're hurt!" "Shhh, my lady," he warned, "Not so loud, that wretched creature could be back at any moment." Serena nervously looked at the door, and then back at the injured man. "Who are you?" she asked, "Why are you here? We have to get out of here!" "Please calm yourself, my lady. My name is Herald, my uncle is a wizard named Sagacity…." Serena gasped. "You've heard of him?" asked Herald. "Why yes, of course," replied Serena. I've never met him, but I've heard great things about him." Herald smiled, "Thank you, he taught me everything I know." "So, you're a wizard?" asked Serena. "I'm a Rawk." "Oh," said Serena, "So you can turn into a raven or a hawk, you're an avian wizard."

"Yes," admitted Herald sadly, until I was kidnapped by the same awful creature that brought you here. I tried to fight him, and that's when he broke my wing. I was in bird form when I tried to get away. I've been searching for my uncle, he has gone missing. When I was accosted, there were two of them. I had just left Wickardia, where I was learning some candle magic from the Wickets. When my lesson was finished, I assembled my pack for a journey to Beauteous, to visit the king and queen. The queen wanted some lavender candles, and I also was to take some herbal remedies to keep at the castle, as the supplies were running low. Soldiers were constantly getting nicked during sword fighting practice, and so on." Serena smiled and nodded for him to go on. He took a sip of water and continued, "Just as I started on the path, the sky became extremely dark. Then I heard a loud popping sound and when I turned around there were these two wolf-like creatures staring at me. Not entirely wolf, half something else. They smelled foul, and I gagged, and grabbed for my wand. One of them knocked it out of my hand, and I morphed into a hawk, to try and fly away, but the other one flew up, they also have wings, and we started fighting. Serena shuddered, "Please, don't tell me anymore, and that's how you're wing was broken?" "In a nutshell, yes, Herald replied, then I felt them lift me up, and before I knew it, I was here, but I was coming to before they descended, and didn't let on. I heard them talking, and the kingdom is in danger. Quagmire is alive and has been in hiding. These evil wolf creatures are his minions. The Murk brothers have been protecting Quagmire, waiting for the chance to take over the kingdom. It's not bad enough they destroyed Ralliant! They plan on keeping us here, just giving us bread and water, to keep us weak, until they have who they want here, and then they will torture us unless we give them our secrets. They're planning on capturing every powerful witch and wizard in all four lands…." "Leaving the king and queen vulnerable, as well!" interrupted Serena. We have to get out of here! Do you have any magic at all, anything we can use to escape?" she asked him fervently. He smirked and reached into his boot, "My lady, being those two creatures aren't too bright, and never checked to see if I had anything on me, I was able to hold onto this small bottle of fog blasts, but, since I am injured, I haven't had much use for them. Just the bottle and the small dagger I gave you to cut your binds. Serena threw up her hands in despair. "My lady,"…Herald began, but Serena interrupted, "Please, call me Serena." "Serena, he said, and then repeated,

Serena, what a beautiful name." Serena smiled, "I know what you are thinking, she said, I'm half human, I'm not that powerful, not that these dolts who captured us would know that. My magic works best at Dragoness, I'm still learning. Wait!"She almost yelled, and then looked worriedly at the door.

She lowered her voice, "I just remembered, I have a healing potion in my amulet!" Herald sat up straighter, "Do you think?" She nodded, "If I can remember the correct spell, I may be able to heal your wing, I have used it before, so I know it works. I'm half feeler. I can heal, I'm not good at combat." she looked down at her hands. My lad…Serena, look at me. "You can trust me, I promise you." Serena looked into his deep green eyes, and instantly felt more at ease. The avian wizard went on, "If you heal my arm, when those two idiots come back, I can temporarily blind them with the fog blasts, and turn into a hawk. I'll hold onto you, and we can fly out of here. We have to warn as many people as we can, and come up with a plan of attack. Serena looked worried, "But will you be strong enough to carry me, and fly." With his left hand, he lifted Serena's chin, "When I first saw your beautiful face, I immediately gained strength."

Serena blushed, and laughed, "Well, we better get started then, and thank you." Serena took off her amulet, and quickly opened the back. She had Herald lie still as she held the tiny bottle over his arm and as she released the contents she repeated the words, "Healing powers, come to light, save Herald from this plight, successfully mend his broken arm, restore him, I ask, of this charm, as I will so mote it be!" There was a small pop of purple smoke and Herald opened his eyes and sat up. He smiled, "You did it, good as new!" He waved his arm about, and pulled Serena into a hug. She looked up at him, and their lips touched. He kissed her tenderly, and suddenly, they both heard loud footsteps. "Get ready," the young wizard hissed, "This is it."

Raven was in back of the potions shop practicing telekinesis defense against attacks, with Stark. "That's great Raven!" complemented the elder, "Now try the…." he was interrupted by Willow who was pacing the floor and threw up her hands, "Oh, what is taking them so long to get those supplies!" Raven walked over to her mother and wrapped her arms around her in a hug, "Mom, I'm worried about Ruby too." Stark was about to say something when Kerina walked in with a few of her wicket guards. "Finally," Willow whispered under her breath. Kerina and the other wickets placed the supplies on the wobbly wooden table that was damaged during the kidnapping. Stark took a big cauldron from the stock of pots in the back and started a fire in the hearth. While they waited for the cauldron to heat up, they discussed what their next move would be. Raven, making a face, picked up what appeared to be dried up shoe leather.

"What is *this*?" she questioned. "Bright Beetle Dung," replied Kerina, with a smirk. "Eww!" exclaimed Raven, "We don't have to *drink* this concoction, do we?" Willow laughed, "No dear, it's not for drinking." Raven wrinkled her nose, "Thank goodness!" Kerina guffawed, "Aw, you should have kept her going for a while!" Stark smirked, Okay ladies, I believe this cauldron is hot enough. Willow and Kerina placed the bright beetle dung, tree sap, azurite crystals, (used for insight), and mushroom oil in the pot. Kerina started the incantation, "The full moon is bright, and we need the sight, make it clear for us to see those who are dear, we need the sight to make things right, we ask this with pure hearts, please give us your light." Raven jumped back as a huge puff of smoke erupted from the cauldron. Then she giggled nervously. Willow gave her a stern look, "Shhhh!' she admonished. Suddenly the liquid in the big pot turned clear, and they could see a big black bird soaring in the sky, then, Raven gasped. Serena was being carried by the tremendous bird! Stark became angry and stamped his foot down hard. Kerina put her hand up, "Stop it, all of you!" she scolded, "She is not harmed, that is no ordinary bird, he's half human. I'm certain he's a wizard." "Oh?" questioned Stark, "and who might he be? How do we know if he is on our side or if he sides with our enemies?" "Quiet!"

scolded Kerina again, "There's something else showing!" The liquid went dark gray, and even Kerina gasped at what they saw next. Emerging from a deep, mountain like cave emerged the head of a dragon; its flaring nostrils snorting and its orange eyes flashing angrily around. A deafening roar spewed from his hideous mouth. Everyone in the room covered their ears at the dreadful sound as the cauldron shook. Stark pushed the women back from the hearth as the big pot started cracking, and then exploded, leaving nothing but a pile of black dust. Kerina fell to her knees, "A warning," she frowned, he's back, and he's coming for us."

When they awoke, Gregor said, "Mmmm, I smell food!" "I'm pretty hungry myself," yawned Ruby, "Hey, where is everybody?" Adorna appeared out of nowhere, and said, "Good morning," I assume you both slept well?" "Yes, and I'm starved!" both teenagers replied in unison. Adorna laughed, "Well go and refresh yourselves at the brook behind that plum tree, and then get yourselves some breakfast, we have a long journey ahead. Oh, and do not attempt to pick any of those plums, the tree is enchanted, not ripe yet, and you do *not* want to perturb it!" Ruby and Gregor looked at each other and shrugged, and then they ran off to wash up. After a hearty breakfast, the group packed up, and Radkiel took out an old looking map, from his backpack.

Thaddeus looked over his shoulder at the map, and remarked, "Here," as he waved his wand over the map, "Now it's updated." Radkiel raise his eyebrows, "Nice trick." Thaddeus tilted his head back and chortled, "It's not that simple, look." "Whoa, what is that?" Adorna exclaimed as she pointed to a big dark space on the map. Everyone looked at the map, perplexed. "All is not being revealed,' said Thaddeus,"Ah, and there's ruins at the bottom. We have to find someone to translate these ruins, and decipher the rest of the map, it's like there is a shadow over it."

"Come," said Radkiel, I only know of one being who can decode this diagram." "Following Radkiel, the group started up the side of the mountain. There were little homes here and there, and they were careful not to intrude on someone's property. People nodded greetings to them, but kept to themselves. Once they came to a clearing near a grand tree with cherry blossoms, Radkiel announced, "Here we are!" Everyone looked around in confusion, and Ruby said, "Um, there's nothing here but a big tree and some bushes." Then she screamed in surprised, "Aaaah!" "Who is trespassing on my village?" came a voice, and then to the visitor's surprise, a head popped out of the ground. "Pappa gnome, greetings!" saluted Radkiel. "Ah, young Radkiel!" bellowed the gnome, as the rest of him popped up from the ground. "Radkiel rifled his hand through his hair which was starting to gray at the temples, "Not so young anymore," he joked. The elder gnome guffawed loudly then said, "I see you've brought visitors." "We need your help sir," Adorna spoke up, "There is unspeakable evil upon us, and…. The wise gnome put up his hand, "I know why you are here, and there have been whispers up and down the mountain." "Of course we will help you, follow me, first we feast." Gregor was about to say they had already eaten when Radkiel stepped on his foot and shot him a look. "Ow!" Gregor bellowed. Everyone looked at him, "Sorry, I stepped on a stone." Radkiel smirked as they followed the elder gnome into the gnome village. As they started walking, the village and everything in it became visible to them. Ruby looked around in amazement at the quaint little gnome homes, and whimsical creatures. The village was beautifully maintained with lush green meadows, and colorful flowers. There were gnomes everywhere; some selling wares, others wheeling flowers in big wheelbarrows to be planted, and some tending to vegetable gardens.

When they arrived to Pappas's house, he yodeled and a pretty female gnome popped her head out of an upstairs window in the enormous tree house. "Doodley doo!" giggled the cheery gnome. "Gerlinda, we have guests," and some business to discuss. Seeing the serious look on all of their faces, Gerlinda quickly came down to greet and welcome the guests. "Oh," said Ruby, it's a lot bigger in here than it looks outside." Gerlinda led them to a huge table and told them to make themselves at home. After she brought out some delicious looking dishes, she sat next to the elder gnome who then spoke, "For those of you who don't know me, my name is Buckram, but my friends call me pappa, this is my bride, Gerlinda. Gerlinda nodded and blushed. She was the same age as Buckram, but looked more youthful, as her counterpart had a long bushy beard; most of the older male gnomes did. Introductions were made all around, and then they enjoyed the luscious food, and talked about the chaos that was going on. When the table was cleared everyone sat back down, Radkiel took out the map. Gerlinda gave pappa his special, but peculiar looking spectacles; they had little wipers on them. "I invented them myself," Pappa said when he noticed the quizzical looks on their faces. Then the wise gnome murmured some unintelligible words and rainbow colored lights exuded from the strange looking glasses. He gave a start, "Oh my," and he clucked his tongue, "This isn't good at all, no no no, not good at all!" Thaddeus cupped his face in his hands. "What is it?" demanded Radkiel, as Gregor grabbed Ruby's hand under the table. "It's Quag-mire," replied pappa. "He's growing stronger by the minute and about these ruins, there is a missing stone, an onyx. It belongs on Prince Edrikal's trident. It shows that the onyx completes the trident and is the only weapon that can defeat

Quagmire." Ruby stood up, "Wait! *Prince* Edrickal? My father was a prince?"

Pappa looked up at the faces around the table. Adorna's was red, Gregor looked as shocked as Ruby, and both Radkiel and Thaddeus looked like they wanted to disappear. "You didn't know, child?" Pappa asked Ruby. "No!" Ruby shouted, "I didn't know, how could that be?" Adorna said gently, "Ruby please sit down, we are not home." Realizing where she was, Ruby apologized for the outburst, and took her seat. Adorna covered Ruby's hands with her own, sighed, and revealed, "Edrical was King Edgeworth's brother." Gregor made a weird sound in his throat, and Radkiel coughed. "You all knew this?" whispered Ruby in astonishment. "I…I didn't know," squeaked out Gregor. As Ruby's eyes filled with tears, Gerlinda gave her a cloth to wipe her eyes, and she patted her back. Then pappa nodded at his wife, and she said, "Excuse me while I get us some tea. "Gregor," said Thaddeus, why don't you help Gerlinda with the tea." Gregor nodded and followed the kind gnome into the kitchen. Radkiel looked at Ruby, "It was for Raven's and your protection. Your father didn't want you to know. Since he chose to become a wizard, he could never inherit the crown and he felt if you knew it would endanger your lives. "But he had no right," frowned Ruby, he pretty much decided our lives for us, what if we wanted to go to court, and serve the king and queen?" Adorna said, "Is that what you would have wanted, to be a princess, and live at the castle?" Ruby spoke right up, "No," that's not for me, but I still should have had that choice!" "Ahem," Pappa cleared his throat, "I am sorry you found out this way young lady, but we have to finish deciphering this map and get you all on your way." Ruby looked into her Godmother's eyes, "I'm okay, it was a shock." Gerlinda and Gregor walked in with a pot of aromatic tea, and some appetizing looking biscuits. While they sipped the delicious tea, Pappa said, "Okay, I'm going to give you some things to take with you. You need to see the green goddess because she is the only one who might be able to help you locate the onyx, and I hope you have someone guarding that trident. This book is called a 'Spellis Writ,' and you will need it as you travel up the mountain. There are spells in here that you will be useful, especially to get past the mountain mums. "What are Mountain Mums?" asked Gregor. Gerlinda answered, "For the most part, they are humble creatures, and they resemble gophers, but they are introverts and pranksters. They do not like trespassers, and they keep to themselves. They will not purposely cause harm, but they may give you trouble, and there is no way around them." Thaddeus asked, "Could I use a sleeping spell on them so we may sneak through their territory?" Pappa raised his eyebrows, "Excellent idea, that settles that!

Next, you are going to need my mystical telescope." Pappa took a big pouch out of a drawer in the wall, and laid it on the table. Almost immediately, a long sparkly object flew out of the bag and landed in front of Gregor. "What the…?" Gregor blinked and opened his mouth but nothing came out. Gerlinda giggled, "Well now, she certainly picked who she wants to be responsible for her!" A little giggle erupted from the enchanted telescope. Adorna smirked as Pappa waggled his finger at Gregor, "Young man, you take good care of Telli, I expect her back, in one piece! Do you have anything to give Isoldina, although I expect she will be a little tough to talk to, under the circumstances." "I have some special candles I brought from the wickets," said Ruby, "I've heard she enjoys the scent of lavender." Gerlinda handed her a basket full of biscuits, "Take these to her also, she adores my raspberry jelly biscuits." Ruby smiled and thanked Gerlinda. Then Gerlinda gave Adorna another basket filled with food, for their journey, and had their water canteens filled. "As you know," said Pappa, "When Ralliant was taken over, by the Murk brothers, most of the survivors fled here, to Shimrock Mountain. It was just about the time that Isoldina inherited the mountain from King Edgeworth. For the most part, the people and creatures that inhabit the mountain are pure of heart, but, there could be unfriendly inhabitants we do not know about who have snuck in by some magic portal or such. The goddess normally keeps up well with the guards and we all have methods to protect our homes, but you can never be too careful, especially, with the recent turn of events, and everything you've told me. There is a protection enchantment on this village, since the gnome village is known for having and manufacturing the most magical articles on the mountain. That is why we were not visible to you when you first arrived, but, my friend Radkiel here remembered the tree, I'd told him about a while back. Even though this is part of the kingdom, you must still be cautious, and be aware of your surroundings. Now, enough of my lecture, we have supplied you with enough food and water for your journey. Go with caution and care. If you need anything else, just whisper it to Telli. She'll get word back to me." Gerlinda gave them a wagon to carry their supplies, and she kissed each one of them goodbye with a tear in her eye, "Be safe," she said, gently. Pappa wished them luck, and they returned to the big blossom tree, where they left off, continuing up the mountain.

When Serena and her new friend returned to dragoness, she noticed a slight darkness to the sky, and how quiet it seemed. "I don't like this," she said aloud. They walked up to the potions shop and the door flew open. Herald stepped in front of Serena and pulled out his sword. Stark emerged, and seeing Herald, pulled out *his* sword and took a fighting stance. "No!" screamed Serena. Both men looked at her but neither one moved. Looking at the two of them, Serena burst out laughing. "Serena, has this…this, creature hurt you?"demanded Stark. Herald had forgotten his wings were still out and he retracted them. "This 'creature,' as you call him, saved my life." "Sir, do stand down," started Herald," I mean no harm, I came here to help, and as you can see, the lady is exhausted." At that, Serena fainted, and Herald caught her just as she was about to hit the ground. Stark ran over to help Herald and apologized for his rudeness. "It's understandable under the circumstances," replied Herald generously, "Let's get her inside, and I'll tell you about our captors, and our passage back here.

After Serena had some tea, made by Daffilda, and she'd rested, she felt much better. She marveled at how well the shop looked, despite the attack and the damage that was done. She told everyone what happened after she was captured and how she and Herald escaped. "We're so happy you are safe," Ruby said, as she ran over and hugged Serena. Willow set down some fruit and cheese, and everyone gathered around to discuss the previous events and how to proceed, as they ate. "I sent for Callioth and Harmonia," said Willow. I'm sure they will be able to sense how the others are doing." Serena stood up, "I feel much better now, thank you all for what you've done to repair the shop." She blinked back tears and Herald placed his hand gently on her shoulder. Willow's eyebrows shot up, and she smiled. Stark looked annoyed as he said, "Well, what is the plan? We don't want to get blindsided." Just then, Callioth and Harmonia arrived with Phinnia, Kerina, and Crizal. Crizal brought elderberry wine from the Dotted Elm, and Kerina brought raspberry scones. Phinnia, not to come empty handed brought her soothing hot chocolate elixir, made with fresh ground cinnamon. When the newcomers were settled, Callioth spoke, "I received a telepathic message from Thaddeus." Everyone sat up straighter in anticipation. "They are all safe, and on their way up the mountain. They received some mystical elements from the gnomes, to assist them through their travel. They also learned some disturbing information. They had the map of navitor with them, and Thaddeus updated it. There was ancient writing on it, ruins to be exact. Buckram, the elder gnome, was able to decipher it and…" Suddenly there was a loud crack of thunder, and Callioth grabbed his forehead as he felt a sharp pain. Everyone jumped up and looked around furtively, while Harmonia tended to Callioth. There was a loud crash outside and Stark ran out with Herald at his heels, to see what the noise was, "Stay here!" Stark yelled to Willow and Raven. Raven started to go after him, but Willow stopped her. Then something crashed into the window and broke the glass. Raven screamed, and Phinnia flew out the door.

"Shhhhh," whispered Adorna as they crept along a winding stony path, "I think we are entering mountain mum territory." They heard loud chuckling and singing. No one moved as they listened to merry sounding mums, who looked like groundhogs except for their purple eyes. "Ouch!" yelled Ruby. "Shhhhh!" admonished Radkiel. "Someone pulled my hair!" rasped Ruby in an annoyed tone. She shot Gregor a look. "Don't look at me," he replied, my hands are full," he said as he gestured to all the loot he was carrying. "Yow!" complained Gregor, "Someone just kicked me!" "If you two don't stop this…" started Radkiel as something kicked the back of his leg, and he stumbled forward. Adorna giggled and then gasped as she saw two purple eyes staring at her, with no body. "Ooh, she pretty." came a voice out of nowhere. "Why you!" said Radkiel as he swiped out toward the voice. Pappa hadn't told them the mums could turn invisible. Thaddeus chortled and said in a low voice, "*We may as well attract them to us, and then I can start the spell.*" He took out the 'Spellis Writ,' Pappa gave him and found the spell he needed. Ruby took one of Gerlinda's raspberry jelly biscuits and waved it around in the air," Mmmm, these raspberry jelly biscuits are so yummy!" Quick as a flash a horde of purple eyes appeared, and then their furry little bodies became visible. "They're actually kind of cute," whispered Ruby as she started tearing off pieces of biscuits to give to the mums. While they were busy munching, Thaddeus took out his wand. After he saw all of the little critters finished their snack, and were clamoring for more, Thaddeus pointed to the creatures and said, "Slumberous Allorous, no trouble comes before us!" and the mums all fell fast asleep in the grass. Ruby giggled as they snuck past, "For little ones, they sure snore loudly!"

Once they were a little more ahead, the group stopped to have a snack and drink water. "How are you holding up?" Radkiel asked Adorna. She smiled, "I'll admit I'm tired, but I'm more worried than anything else. Ruby came running over to them, "Hurry; there's something wrong with Thaddeus!" Gregor was holding the writhing man up, "I don't know what happened, all of a sudden he screamed out in pain and grabbed his head!" Radkiel and Adorna tried to calm the feeler as he shook and held his head. He collapsed into their arms, and tried to talk. Adorna gave him some water and Radkiel said, "Take it slow Thaddeus, what did you see?"

"Dark…ness," he sputtered out, "St…storm…" and then he passed out.

Part Two

Raven ran out after Phinnia, "Nooo, Raven, come back!" cried Willow. Willow and the others all ran out, wands and weapons in hand. They saw Raven fighting off a winged beast with her sword, and Willow cast a lightning bolt at the beast. Stark was standing over Herald who was wounded on the ground. Serena ran over, "No!" she cried, as tears formed in her eyes. Stark looked at her and realized she was in love with the injured man. He felt guilty for having misjudged him, but then he shook it off. "Serena, he'll be okay, it's just a small cut." Serena looked at Stark gratefully and nodded, "Go help the others." Stark ran in front of Raven and stabbed at the beast with his sword. When it evaporated, another appeared. There were six in total. Phinnia and Daffilda cast a spell together and the last two creatures turned to stone.

Willow flicked her wand at them and they crumbled into dust. "Whew," Raven was trying to catch her breath, "What is going on?" Harmonia went over to Herald with a healing poultice for his wound, "*That,* was another warning. Quagmire must be getting stronger. Let's hope that Adorna, Radkiel, and the others get back to Dragoness soon or the whole kingdom will be in danger of the dragon's wrath." "I don't understand," replied Raven, "I thought those years ago, our people got along with the dragons and we were all at peace, what changed?" Stark answered as he helped Herald to his feet, "Unfortunately, we won't know that until the others get back. The Murk brothers must have gotten hold of Quagmire as a baby, and had stolen his egg. Then, they raised him to become evil. It's the only answer I can come up with without knowing all of the facts." Calioth replied, "I have a feeling you are correct in your assumption, Stark," she looked at the sky, "It's getting dark, let's go back inside and prepare ourselves in case there's another attack."

At Murk Island, at the bottom of a volcano, was Quagmire's lair. The volcano wasn't active, well, unless someone or *something*, decided to activate it. Nefari laughed as his brother related to him how his minions injured the wizard Herald. "That's the least of those loathsome idiots' problems," Querd hissed. Quagmire opened one eye and yawned. The two brothers jumped out of the way as flames shot out of the napping dragon's nostrils, "You're disturbing my sleep!" the annoyed beast hissed. Panting, Nefari replied,

"All you do is sleep, while we do all the work." Quagmire went to open his mouth again, and Querd put his hands up to cover his face as he cowered, "Okay okay, don't get into a snit!" "Fools!" hissed the dragon, "You're wasting time, you should be hunting for the onyx, and the other eggs, before someone else beats you to it, and if that happens…" Querd gulped, "That's not going to happen, no one else knows about the other dragon eggs." Quagmire grinned so wickedly, that both brothers stepped back, "You two underestimate the powers of those you do not understand, we are not dealing with amateurs. Your ineffective tricks have not been faring well. A wizard was able to escape the tower with a witch!" The angry dragon swished his huge tail, and the brothers grabbed onto each other as the ground shook. Nefari replied, "Master, we are saving the best for battle. We are just giving them a taste for what is to come." Querd nodded in agreement. "I suggest," roared the impatient beast, "that you imbeciles go on the quest yourselves to find those eggs, instead of those dim-witted puppets you call, 'warriors!' The hot breath of wind from the angry dragon almost blew their hair off their heads. "And I mean NOW!" The Murk brothers looked at each other and Querd spoke up, "Whatever you say, Quagmire, please have patience." The dragon started to grin again, as he lifted his head, and the brothers took off, without looking back.

Thaddeus was feeling much better and sat up, "I fear we need to hurry our journey, something is amiss at Dragoness, there's been trouble, and I can feel Quagmire's anger. He grows more impatient with every moment." Ruby said, "If the Murk brothers are so powerful, how come they haven't just attacked us outright? What is stopping them?" Thaddeus grinned, "Ah, that's just it, they may be powerful, in their own right, but neither of them is too bright. Their skills aren't honed. They are very lazy and do not practice as we all do. They want glory and do not want to work for it. This is why Quagmire grows angrier and more impatient; he was brought up by two evil, self righteous, conceited beings. When their parents, were killed, they no longer had anyone to instruct them or teach them how to fight. All of the evil beings that had served Dracha and Xenos abandoned them, and their supposed aunt, Iniquitous, didn't have much use for them. She had her own agenda. The twins have been getting by with the evil creatures they've created at the flick of their ill- fated wands, by performing substandard spells. Quagmire was a much younger dragon when his mistress was killed. After her death, he only had the brothers to, let's say, care for him. My belief is that the brothers want to take over the kingdom, but intend on Quagmire doing it for them." Suddenly Radkiel whispered, "Quiet, I hear rustling." Everyone stood on guard, listening. Adorna shivered as she felt a chill up her spine. "I feel like we're being watched," she whispered back. "Everyone stays close to me," Radkiel said, as he led the way higher into the mountain. Ruby screamed,"AAAAHHHH!" Gregor whipped around ready to pounce, and then he started laughing. A fluffy brown owl was perched on Ruby's shoulder, its bright topaz colored eyes blinking furiously. "What the…" started Ruby, with a nervous giggle. "I was going to tell you this later," said Adorna, "You're to be an Avian wizard." "But, I'm a witch," protested Ruby. "True," agreed Radkiel, but you are only half witch. You get your wizardry skills from your father." Ruby's mouth fell open, as did Gregor's. "I really wish I was made aware of these things ahead of time!" huffed the teen. "I completely understand, soothed Adorna, but these were all things that were going to be revealed to you on your eighteenth birthday. Just like Raven's powers were revealed to her. Unfortunately, your revelations are coming a little earlier than expected because of the attack on the kingdom. Thaddeus reminded them of their new feathered friend, "This lovely bird seems to have a message for us." In one of the owl's claws, there was a curled up message. "Go ahead Ruby, open it," encouraged Adorna. Ruby's hand trembled as she reached for the note.

The beautiful owl willingly lifted his claw and released the note into Ruby's hand. He blinked at her, as he watched her open it. Ruby read the words to herself, and then cleared her throat, "It says, my dear child, I bestow this gift upon you, his name is Boon, he will help light the rest of the way up the mountain. I cannot leave my post as I need to see to all goings on throughout the mountain. Have no fear, you are welcome here, but heed this warning, make haste as time is running out…" Ruby wiped a tear from her eye as she pet the animal's head. It made a noise that sounded like purring. Radkiel smiled, "Well Ruby it looks like you have your familiar." A familiar was a term used for a witches' pet. "The threat must be serious if Isoldina is able to put aside her disdain from the past." "Let us not waste another moment," said Thaddeus, "Onward and upward."

The ugly vulture flew down and landed on Quagmire's neck. "Ah, my friend," said the foul breathed dragon, "What news do you bring me?" The bird squawked and hissed, "The sister's powers grow stronger. They are vigorous in their training and will soon be guided by the green goddess." "Yesss, that is to be expected, ranted Quagmire, I need to find those dragon eggs and the black stone before they do. If they get to them first…, he slammed down his tail in a rage, as he squeezed the vulture's skinny neck, "We all lose!"

Gregor took off his shoe to take a stone out of it, and rubbed his sore foot, "Can't we stop for a while," he complained, "I'm getting tired." Ruby shot him a dirty look.

"What?" he asked her in disbelief, "You're not tired?" She retorted, "I *am*, but I wasn't going to say anything."

"Okay, so *you're* better than me!" Gregor shot back. Ruby's eye started twitching. Adorna clapped her hands, "Please! We are all tired, and I'm guessing hungry too. "We'll stop at the next spring or brook, and rest a bit." Thaddeus said, "Up ahead, I hear a waterfall." Gregor took off his backpack and placed it on the ground. Abruptly, he jumped as his bag began to move. He pointed and yelled, "Hey, there's something moving in there!" Radkiel took his Wizard's staff and poked at the bag. "Owwie, owwie!" a voice screeched, and then a little head with purple eyes popped out of the bag. "A mountain mum!" giggled Ruby. "How did it get in my pack?" wondered Gregor, as he scratched his head. "It's a baby," remarked Adorna. "What are we going to do with it," groused Radkiel, "We have no time to return it to its home." Thaddeus replied, "We will have to take it with us, we can return him or her, after our business with the goddess is completed." Ruby gently picked up the furry creature and cradled it in her arms. Her new familiar didn't look pleased, and let out a screech. Ruby smirked and scolded; "Now don't you be jealous, Boon, after all, it's only a baby, and you and I just met!" The beautiful bird cast his eyes down, and Ruby ruffled his feathers, "Besides, you are *much* more mature than this little babe, and I'll need your help to keep it out of trouble." At that, the owl puffed out his chest proudly." Thaddeus tried not to laugh. "Now that that's settled," said Adorna, can we please continue? I am starting to feel uneasy." "As am I," replied Thaddeus, sounding worried.

After everyone had some water and a snack, they continued up the mountain. Radkiel put his hand up, "Stop!" Ruby began, "What…" "Thaddeus yelled, "Get down!" Everyone ducked down and crawled behind a big rock. Thaddeus took out his wand, ready to strike at any moment.

Suddenly they heard a loud screech; it was coming from above them, in the sky. "Ruby, guard the mum," hissed Thaddeus, vultures are known to eat small animals." Ruby hid the little mum in her backpack and held it tight to her body. Gregor took out his sword and stood in front of Ruby. Adorna cast a bubble around them to keep the vulture away from them. Sludge, the black vulture, swooped down and tried to penetrate the bubble but failed. "Maybe I cannot get to you now," Croaked the filthy bird of prey, but soon you will feel the wrath of Quagmire!" The feathered enemy continued, "You've been warned!" Boon tried to fly up, but bounced back, forgetting about the bubble. "Boon no!" cried Ruby. Gregor pushed her back. The owl flew back to Ruby and stood on her shoulder. "Ha!" the cruel vulture cackled, "That talentless fowl thinks he can hurt me!"

Boon's feathers bristled as Ruby held his feet down on her shoulder. She whispered to him, "Ignore that excrement, he cannot hold a Wicket's candle to you!" Radkiel, not wanting to break the protective bubble yelled, "Be gone you vile rot, before I zap you into oblivion!" The filthy bird squawked again, "You've been warned," and he took off. Waiting a few moments to make sure he was really gone, Adorna released the spell, and the bubble evaporated. Radkiel stepped out and looked around, "He's gone." Gregor asked, "How did he get here in the first place, I thought we were pretty safe here." "We are not safe anywhere right now," surmised Thaddeus, "In fact, we are in more danger than we ever were before."

"How are you feeling sir," asked Phinnia. "Please, call me Herald," said their new friend, "There is no need to address me formally, we are equals." Phinnia was both touched and startled by his genuineness, and she curtsied. Herald looked at her, and she blushed, then they both laughed. Raven had called out, "Come and eat!" Willow, Raven and Daffilda prepared a warm, hearty meal and set the table in the training room of the potions shop in a cheerful manner. Queen Kerina brought some beautiful flowers from the troll gardens to decorate the table, and add some relaxing scents to the room. Everyone was quiet as they served themselves the yummy meal of shepherd's pie, biscuits with elderberry jam, corn on the cob, and Kerina's special herb salad. For dessert they had prickle pear pudding, which was very rich, but tasty.

Everyone was very hungry, and there was silence as they enjoyed the meal. When the table was cleared, and everything was put away, they sat back down to discuss where they should go from there. Stark spoke up first, "I don't know about anyone else, but I think we should either plan on meeting up with the others, or we stay here and conjure up every defensive spell, weapon, and army, we can muster." Phinnia said as she raised her brow, "If we depart to meet up with the others, we leave Dragoness vulnerable, I don't like it!" She stamped her foot. "As much as I want to be with my sister, I have to agree with Phinnia," replied Raven sadly. Everyone jumped as Kerina slammed her small hand on the table, "This is nonsense, utter nonsense! What we need is a solid plan, we need to figure out a way to draw that nasty dragon and those horrid Murk brothers into a trap, and then, we take care of them once and for all, and good riddance!" She thundered. Willow was shocked that such loud sound could come from the little wicket. She smiled, "Well, we have a few different ideas here; we will have to vote on them, to be fair."

"Never mind what's fair, sister!" Retorted Stark, "We need to do what's right, what's going to protect us and our kingdom!" "Might I make a suggestion," asked Harmonia. Everyone turned to face the feeler. "I propose that Callioth, Serena, Willow, and I make another seeing potion, to determine if we can get a vision of where the others are at, or if Callioth or I could connect with Thaddeus. In the mean time, the rest of you could follow the second idea Stark had and start gathering up supplies, and an army, so we can be ready for another attack. We are seriously running out of time, I can feel it." Serena looked around the table, "All agreed?" Everyone nodded, and Herald said, "I can help Stark gather an army, but we will need to venture to Beauteous." Serena touched his shoulder and he smiled, "It's okay, I am almost as good as new."

Stark smiled grimly, "Then we start at once." Herald turned himself into a large eagle and Stark pointed his own wand at himself and said, "Minutia!" Then he took his smaller self, climbed onto the avian wizard's back, and they took off.

"Whew, that was scary!" exclaimed Ruby. Then she smiled as the cute little mum baby cuddled closer to her. Boon made a noise and fluttered his wings to show his annoyance at the small creature. Ruby was about to scold him when Gregor said, "Shhh! what is that now?"

Everyone listened, then Radkiel said in an annoyed tone, "I don't hear anything." "Oh," exclaimed Adorna, "I hear it," she pointed to Gregor's backpack. "Not again," groaned Gregor. "I hope you do not have another little furry creature in there," replied Thaddeus. Suddenly, the flap of the backpack shot open and a long piece of metal stuck out. Then they heard a small giggle. Gregor smacked his forehead, "Telli, I've forgotten all about you!" The enchanted telescope grunted in disapproval. Ruby smirked, "I think you hurt her feelings." Gregor carefully took the ornate object out of his bag, and apologized to it. Radkiel tried not to laugh as Adorna gave him a dirty look. "She's doing something." Gregor whispered. The odd telescope sounded like it was crunching glass as it switched lenses and moved its gears. "I think she's trying to show us something," Gregor surmised with a dumbfounded look on his face. "Well, look into it!" said Ruby excitedly. Gregor looked nervously at the others as they urged him on, and then he looked at their surroundings. Worried that they would never reach the top of the mountain, and deciding they needed all the help they could get, he closed his left eye, looked into Telli with his right, and then he gasped. He almost dropped the enchanted object as he pointed toward the top of the mountain. "What?!" Everyone shouted at once. Even Boon screeched in annoyance. Ruby couldn't take it anymore and she grabbed the telescope out of Gregor's hand, and looked through it. "Oh," she shouted happily, "I see it, it's the top of the mountain, and it's beautiful! If you keep looking through the telescope there are silver arrows that point out the way, if you take away the telescope, you can't see it though. Oh, and there's something else! There's a beautiful multicolored bird." Gregor tried to take the telescope back, but Ruby slapped his hand away, "She's spelling something out, with birdseed, Oh but it's in ruin code."

"Wait, "exclaimed Thaddeus, Do not put the telescope down or you will lose the vision, Pappa gave me the ruin alphabet in case we needed it for the map, I will take it out, and help you decipher the message. The message read, "Take heed when following these last few steps, enemies around will impede your reps, look to the map and the lighted ways, nothing is as it seems these days." Thaddeus cried out as if in pain, and Adorna ran to his side, "What is it?" she said gently. "Something is not right. That message is a warning. We have to look out for, he gasped, an imposter!" The group looked at each other stunned, and then they all began to talk at once. "Quiet!" yelled Radkiel, "We have to think about this. Who could be the imposter and ..." Telli started making noise again and shifted into a round shape, almost like a crystal ball.

Thaddeus gently took it from Ruby's shaking hands, and set it down. Everyone sat down around it and their jaws dropped at what they were seeing. When the fog cleared from the glass, they saw a vision; it was Isoldina and Sagacity, the missing wizard, both looking worn and sad. They were sitting together in a dark cave and it looked like their hands and feet were bound. They both looked defeated as they tried to loosen their binds, and called out for help. Then the vision abruptly disappeared. Telli turned back into a telescope, and flew to Gregor. Now it was Radkiel who smacked himself in the head, "So that's what happened to Sagacity. He's been kidnapped, as well as the green goddess." "How can two such powerful people have been overtaken?" asked Gregor. "There is only one way," surmised Thaddeus, "Sagacity's wand was taken. He had to be with the green goddess at the time, for both of them to be captured."

"Then…Then who is up there?" Ruby pointed, "And who sent Boon to me?" Adorna looked grim, "I don't know who's up there, but we have a decision to make, do we go up there and face whoever the imposter is, or do we go back and get the others and rescue Sagacity and the goddess?"

"Well," the old witch cackled, "Are they coming!" "I don't know grandmother," said Querd. Magpie Murk, the Murk brother's grandmother, smacked her old, crusty lips together as she waggled her crooked finger at him, "You boys will be the death of me!" she laughed and then started hacking. "Ah, it's ready," she cackled again, as she clapped her hands together. "Bring me a mug, you useless wart!" She bellowed. "Querd gave her a mug from his bag. The old hag then scooped up the green liquid from the cauldron she'd been working over and filled the mug to the top. She held it to her lips and said, "Here's spit in your eye!" and she choked down the horrid tasting drink. Querd covered his face and closed his eyes as a big cloud of red smoke appeared and the mug fell to the floor and shattered. When the smoke cleared he opened his eyes and gasped, as there before him stood the green goddess, well, not the real one, but a reasonable facsimile. Luckily, Ambrosia, the goddess' parrot had been outside and remained undetected by the horrid trio. She had had just enough time to send the warning to Ruby and the group before they walked into Magpie's malicious trap. "What's the matter boy," hissed the old witch, "never seen your old granny looking this good, eh!" At that, the wicked warlock turned away in disgust. "Let's get ready for our guests," the fake goddess trilled.

Willow was pacing the floor as she waited for the potion she was making to cool. "Mother please try to calm down," said Raven. "I know you're worried, we all are."

"Yes, but I have a horrible feeling your sister and the others are walking into danger, and I cannot shake it," replied Willow. Phinnia flew in and saw the grim duo. She whispered, "I have news." Since the others were elsewhere doing various tasks, Phinnia pulled the two witches aside to make sure no naysayers were listening and said, "As you know, Daffilda has avian powers. I sent her to Shimrock Mountain to keep an eye on our friends. She was in the form of a blue bird. She went up to the mountain and sensed something was not right. She flew higher and higher, but the higher she went, the less her powers worked for some reason. Anyway, she was able to see into the green goddess' chamber, and the goddess was not there. She found Ambrosia, Isoldina's parrot on top of the roof, and the colorful bird informed her that she was able to warn Ruby and the others not to continue the journey. Then Daffilda peered into the window and one of the Murk brothers was there, with an old witch, whom he called 'grandmother.' Daffilda was so startled she almost gave herself away. She was able to fly down a few feet, and saw Radkiel and the others retreating. What they do from there is up to them though. Daffilda was starting to get weak so I telepathed her to come back, it'll be a little while before she returns." Willow covered her hand with her mouth and let out a little cry, "Magpie Murk!" "Oh no!" exclaimed Phinnia, "That old buzzard is still around?" "Who is Magpie Murk?" Raven asked aloud. "Magpie Murk!" repeated Serena as she walked into the room, after overhearing the name. "Why are you even mentioning that gruesome name?" shuddered the store owner. Raven's nostrils were starting to flair as no one answered her question. "What?" asked Serena when she saw the looks on their faces. Phinnia repeated her story and Serena looked grim as well. Then, seeing how Raven was about to explode, she turned to her and said, "Magpie Murk was an evil sorceress and grandmother of the Murk brothers. She has outlasted numerous battles and was once a very powerful witch. She had been banished from the kingdom some years ago, and no one had heard from her since. We all thought she was dead. The Murk brothers must have been hiding her somewhere." "Who knows how many cretins those two creeps have on their side!" groaned Raven, then she shouted, "Look!" An owl with a small scroll in its claws flew in through the window. It landed on Raven's shoulder. "Ouch!" she exclaimed, "Don't you ever have your claws trimmed?" The owl winked at her, and Raven's jaw dropped. Suddenly the owl flew up and transformed into a human and landed next to her. Raven wobbled and the handsome wizard caught her in his arms. "Sorry for the dramatics," he apologized, "But it was the quickest way to get here, my name is Noble, and I'm a knight of the king and queen." He bowed, "Stark and Herald sent me to let you ladies know that they arrived to Beauteous safely, and they have warned the king and queen of the goings on here. The majesties granted you are to have an army, and Stark and Herald will be back with the army soon. I am to stay on here, if that's okay…" "It's fine by me," Raven burst out. Willow and Serena both giggled, and Raven turned crimson, "What I meant was, the more help, the better." Serena cleared her throat, "Raven, why don't you get this nice young man something to eat, he must be hungry after his journey." Noble smiled, "I don't want you to go to any trouble." "Nonsense," replied Willow, "you two go ahead." The two young people started to walk away when Noble turned and said, "Oh, my lady, I almost forgot, the queen sent a message for you." He handed Willow the scroll of paper, and followed Raven into the kitchen of the back room. Willow opened the small paper with trembling hands. Serena looked over her shoulder and read out loud, "My dear friend Willow, I wish I was writing to you during a happier times. Stark and Herald, have let the king and I know of the dire circumstances of our kingdom. As you know, I lost my powers when I became queen, and that being said, I do still have my instincts, and I've had a feeling there was danger lurking, but could not figure out exactly what it was. We have prepared an army, and are sending Stark and Herald back with said army shortly. Please take care of our son Noble. I sent him on ahead; he has become a great warrior. The king and I will stay here with a smaller group of guards to protect the castle. Please understand we need to be here in case there is an attack on Beauteous. Willow, I am sorry we have not been in touch before this dreadfulness, safe journey my dear friend." Serena put her hand over Willow's as she saw her shed a tear.

"Of course I am not upset with her for staying on at Beateous, but I am annoyed she *hasn't* been in touch before this," said Willow. Serena patted her hand and replied, "Of course, I think we are all a little upset about how things unfolded years ago, but, now is not the time for past regrets, we have a battle to get ready for." "Yes, you are right," sniffed Willow, "Let's get started on those potions!"

Isoldina was getting worried because Sagacity was getting weaker by the minute. Neither one of them had use of their powers on Murk Island. Whatever spell Nefari used on them, which was most likely conjured up by Magpie, was very potent. One minute she was welcoming Sagacity to Shimrock Mountain, and the next, she was waking up on Murk Island, bound and gagged. Sagacity was the oldest and wisest wizard in the kingdom, but he was worn down. It didn't help that the Murk brothers were pretty much starving them, only throwing them an apple here and there and warm water. The worst of it was the fact that they were in Quagmire's lair, and it seemed he always had his eyes on them. If only they could get him to sleep, but then there was his evil vulture counterpart. "All cannot be lost," the green goddess said to herself, "Think, think!" She was startled from her thoughts by the loud growl of Quagmire, and the crush of his tail hitting the ground, "SSSludge!" the dragon hissed, "What news do you have for me?" The creature flew down to his master. Isoldina may have been weak, but her extra sensitive hearing was still in her favor, and she listened fervently to what the moldy bird told Quagmire. "Soooo," replied the fire breather, the king and queen are forming an army, well now, I think we can summon one up as well, don't you think so, my feathered friend?" Sludge babbled, "Master, I don't think…" Quagmire slammed down his enormous tail, "No, you *don't* think! Now, go find those two idiot brothers, and get me an army or you'll be nothing but a pile of feathers when I get through with you!" Sludge made a gurgling sound and flew away. Isoldina smiled, she knew just what she had to do.

They finally reached the top of the mountain. It was eerily quiet, and for a few moments, no one made a sound. Then Radkiel whispered, "We all know what we have to do, correct?"

Everyone nodded. Ruby made sure the sleeping mum was secure in her backpack. Everyone had their wands out, and held them tightly to their bodies. Boon stood bravely on Ruby's shoulder. Radkiel mouthed, "Now!" Adorna and Radkiel stormed the door to the dwelling, and knocked it down. Both of them blinked unbelievingly, when they saw the green goddess turn around and smile. Then Thaddeus bellowed, "It's not her, watch out!" Suddenly, Querd came out of the shadows with his wand drawn. He sent a fireball toward Thaddeus, and Radkiel jumped in front of him and sent it back at Querd who jumped out of the way and laughed.

Adorna quickly fired her wand toward Querd and knocked him down. The imposter then in a raspy angry voice yelled, "How dare you, that's my grandson!" Then the hag sent a lightning bolt toward Adorna. Gregor pushed Adorna out of the way, and pointed his wand toward the witch. Electricity flew back and forth. Magpie started to cough and Radkiel took the opportunity to strike at the old witch. She fell to her knees just as Querd shot a bolt at Radkiel. Ruby couldn't take anymore, and as the fire behind her eyes was unleashed, she hit Querd and he cried out in pain as the flames which kept coming at him, were growing hotter and stronger.

Adorna yelled, "Ruby enough, you'll burn us all down!" Gregor ran over to Ruby and went behind her to gently talk her out of her rage. "We still need him to get to Quagmire," spoke up Thaddeus. At that, Ruby began to calm down. Her hair was wild, and all she could think about was how much she wished her father was there. Magpie, starting to recover, stood up and shot a fireball at Ruby, and it hit her shoulder.

"Ahhh!" cried out Ruby and she went to her knees.

Boon flew over the old wretch and starting pulling her hair with his claws. Gregor and Thaddeus ran over to Ruby as the imposter tried to zap Ruby again. All of a sudden, the little mountain mum popped up out of Ruby's backpack and out of her eyes shot liquid ice, which froze Magpie in her place. Boon had just enough time to fly out of the way, and squawked his annoyance. Then the little ball of fur turned toward Querd who tried to run, but wasn't quick enough, and he too was frozen on the spot. Thaddeus quickly healed Ruby's shoulder with the word, "Curative!" Radkiel Remarked, "Our little friend here has bought us some time," he pet the small animal on the head, "But, we don't know how much, so I suggest we get out of here, and get back to dragoness to help the others." Ruby scooped up her new furry friend and said as she ruffled her furry face, "Well little one, we have something in common, don't we?" Ruby winked at the little mum, who winked back and cooed. "What about these two?" asked Gregor as he pointed to Magpie and Querd. "We'll take care of them later," answered Adorna, "Back down the mountain we go!"

"Sagacity!" whispered Isoldina. She gently shook the old wizard into coherence. "Please, I need to tell you something." Sagacity slowly opened his fevered eyes, and hoarsely whispered, "Yes, my dear, I'm listening." He coughed, and the goddess gave him a drink of the warm water she saved for him. "You have to hold on, the vulture has gone on an errand for the dragon, and my sister, the queen, does not have her powers of sorcery anymore, but, she does still have visions. I think I can connect with her telepathically and let her know where we are. She can send help, and we can get our powers back. Please hold on!" The old wizard nodded and passed out again. Isoldina ripped a piece of cloth from her dress, dipped it in the water, and tried to revive her old friend as she frantically began trying to connect with Queen Primrose, in her mind.

The king and queen were in the middle of sending off Stark and Herald with the army to Dragoness, when the queen suddenly cried out and grabbed her head with both hands. King Edgeworth grabbed the queen and remarked, "My lady, what is it, are you ill?" Stark and Herald both turned around at once. "Ugh," cried the queen, "Please…please wait" Stark and Herald bowed, then Stark said, "Your majesty, how can we help?" "I…I'm getting a vision," she stammered, "I still get them; it's all that's left of the powers I once had." Everyone stood quietly and waited for the queen to continue. She squeezed her eyes shut, and then cried out, "It's Isoldina, she's in trouble, and the missing wizard is with her, and he is very weak….they're," she winced, "They're being held by Quagmire!" "No time to lose," exclaimed the king, "Go to dragoness, and get our kingdom back!"

Willow, Serena, Raven, and Callioth surrounded the cauldron in the fireplace as they chanted. They're eyes were closed as they held hands and swayed back and forth. Callioth opened one eye and whispered, "I'm starting to see something!" As the liquid cleared, the ladies could make out some shapes, and then Raven squealed, "Look, they're coming down the mountain!" "A little worse for wear, I'd say," noticed Willow. "No one appears to be injured," remarked Callioth, "We can be thankful for that!" "Oh," exclaimed Serena, "It's getting dark, we are losing the seeing." "No, wait," replied Callioth, "We are being shown something else; it's getting foggy and gray though." "Oh!" exclaimed Willow, "It's the green goddess!" "Where is she, and who did the others see at Shimrock mountain?" "She looks distressed and wan" whispered Serena. Abruptly the women jumped back as a big ugly head showed in the big pot and an earsplitting wail sounded. Then the cauldron went black. Stunned, from what they had just witnessed, Raven pulled out her wand when Noble walked noisily into the room. Serena grabbed her hand, "Relax," she said gently, "It's Noble, and you don't want to zap *him*."

Startled, Noble said, "I'm sorry my ladies, I hope I didn't interrupt, have you news?" The witches' all looked at each other. Phinnia and Kerina walked in with supplies from the forest, and saw all of the serious faces. "What?" they both asked in unison. "We performed a seeing," replied Callioth, "and what it showed, is worse than we thought. It came into view that Quagmire has somehow captured Isoldina." Phinnia gasped, and her hand went to her mouth.

Callioth continued, "We also saw Adorna and the others making their way down the mountain. It seems like they did some fighting, judging by their disheveled appearances. "If Isoldina was captured, then where is she?" asked Kerina. "That's what we'd all like to know," replied Raven in a concerned voice. Phinnia spoke up, "We have our supplies, so we can start crafting weapons and make elixirs. Kerina has brought her people and has sent word to the wickets that are still on Wickardia." "As per the queen's orders," began Willow, "A small group is to stay behind in each land to procure its safety. We cannot abandon any part of the kingdom for fear of it being taken over by the Murk brothers and the evil dragon." Willow looked at Serena, and Raven picked up on her mother's thoughts. Willow immediately put her fingers to her lips to tell Raven to keep quiet. Raven shook her head in agreement and said out loud, "I'm going to make sure my sword is in order, Callioth, will you come with me please." "I can go with you my lady," said Noble. "You are needed here Noble," said Willow, "I promised your mother you would be here when Stark and Herald returned." "Very well, my lady," he replied to Willow. Raven said she and Callioth would return soon, and they took off to check on the trident.

Callioth put her hand to her mouth as they approached Raven's home. The flowers out front were all dug up and she could see the windows of the house were broken, with glass shards askew. Raven frowned, "We've stayed away too long!" Afraid of what they were going to find inside, they stepped cautiously into the doorway, both with their wands out. "Aaaaaak!" A vulture came tearing at them, but Raven was quick, and stabbed the beast with her sword, wounding him. Unfortunately it was able to get away. As the two women made their way further into the home they shook their heads at the destruction of the once beautiful cottage.

Callioth grabbed Raven's hand, but Raven was too angry to be upset, and shrugged it off. She ran to her bedroom, and saw that the small rug near her bed hadn't been touched. She removed the rug, and Callioth helped her open the trap door, that led to the underground room where the weapons closet was. With trembling hands, Raven waved her wand and mumbled the words, "Release, Reveal, Unconcealed!" The closet door snapped open to reveal the shiny trident. Both ladies let out a breath of relief, and then Raven said, "Thank goodness that bird is an idiot." Suddenly there was a rustling sound, and they both threw up their wands in anticipation. Abruptly, Callioth starting laughing and pointed when Raven looked at her.

There was a small rabbit scurrying away with a large carrot in its mouth. Raven smirked, "Well, someone got what he wanted." Then she became serious, "I think I should stay here, no telling when someone else will be back looking for the trident." "I'm inclined to agree with you, but you shouldn't stay here alone. I'll go back and tell the others what happened, and send Noble to stay with you." Raven smiled for a moment, but then said, "Are you sure we can trust him?"

Callioth replied, "He *is* the majesties' son, why are you having doubts about him?" "I guess because I just met him," Surmised Raven, I don't know him at all." "Did you ever think that maybe he feels the same way, and he came to help us, anyway?" asked Callioth. The teen half smiled, "Since you put it that way, I'll give him a chance, but if he gets out of line..." she put her hand on her sword.

Sludge coughed and wheezed as he flew down to his master, Quagmire. The dragon looked more hostile than ever, "Got yourself nicked, did you!" he growled mercilessly. "Master, I could not find the trident," whispered the wounded bird. "They must have an enchantment guarding it." The dragon roared his displeasure at the news, as he thumped his enormous tail, "I warned you of this, you were not careful, and where are those two imbeciles!" Suddenly a large cloud of smoke appeared, with Magpie and the two brothers behind it. "Your age is showing, old hag!" seethed

Quagmire, "You once were a powerful witch, now you're an aging piece of waste!" "I wouldn't be so cocky," the witch warned, "You have *no* powers because your siblings eggs never hatched, in fact, no one knows where the lost eggs are, so don't you go trying to mock old Maggie!" Querd almost fell over when it seemed like there was an earthquake, suddenly. He grabbed onto his brother and exclaimed, "What's going on!" as the old volcano shook violently.

Isoldina smiled as she held Sagacity's hand, "Help is on the way, my old friend, help is on the way."

Stark, and Herald were back in Dragoness with the king and queen's warriors. They were happily received, rested a bit, and had a hearty meal. One of the warriors took off her helmet, and Stark said in surprise, "You're a woman!" Serena and the other women of dragoness smirked, and Serena replied, "Stark, don't tell me you're a chauvinist?" The young female warrior walked over to Stark as she blew the hair off her face, "And what is your problem with women, sir?" Stark felt all eyes on him, and spied Herald looking amused in the corner. He pleaded with him with his eyes, '*Help Me!*' Herald came forward, "My lady," he bowed, "I think what the gentleman meant was he has never seen such a capable female warrior before, as shown by the many medals on your armor." "Stark smiled gratefully, "Yes my lady, I was astounded by your apparent, admirable achievements." The fair haired woman was so quick, Stark didn't have a chance to react as he found himself knocked on his back with the young woman's foot on his chest and her sword at his throat. Phinnia giggled out loud and Kerina snorted as the young woman said, "Just an example of my,'Admirable Achievements,' as you stated. Then she placed her sword back in the sheath of her tabard, and put her hand out to help Stark up. Herald started laughing, and Stark followed along, as did the rest of the large group. "Well, said Adorna, as she walked into the room, I'm glad you are all in good spirits."

Everyone let out a loud whoop as Ruby, Gregor, Thaddeus and Radkiel followed in behind the expert swordswoman. "Ah, Ornatia, I see you made it here, with the other warriors," Adorna smiled approvingly. Stark's face tinged an awkward pink color as he looked at the floor. After everyone was greeted and updated on the latest developments, the newly arrived group ate and sat down with everyone else. Realizing her sister was not there, Ruby asked, "Where is Raven?" Willow was about to reply, when Callioth bustled into the shop. She had a horrified look on her face, and everyone started questioning her at once. "Stop!" yelled Radkiel," Let her speak." "Raven and I went Willow's to check on the trident, she began, "As we approached the house we noticed the garden was torn up, and the windows were broken. There was glass everywhere, and as we cautiously started into the house, Sludge came after us."

Willow gasped and grabbed Stark's shoulder. Callioth put her hand up, Raven is fine, I cannot say the same for that filthy bird though. She slashed him with her sword, but he managed to fly away, surely back to Murk Island. With your permission Willow, I suggest you send Noble to stay with her to guard the hiding place, as quickly as possible. Ornatia, who was the leader of the king and queen's army said, "A few of my soldiers can go with Noble, I don't think there should only be two people guarding such a valuable weapon, if you don't mind my saying so." Phinnia who was hovering near by cleared her throat, "I appreciate the fact that we have to get ready for a war of sorts, but there are also the matters of the two missing eggs, and the trident's missing stone that need to be cleared up. Don't forget, Daffilda found one egg in the forest, which means there is still one missing. Crizal is hiding the egg at The Spotted Elm." Radkiel spoke up, "And we still have to rescue Isoldina and Sagacity, if he is ill, we don't have much time." "I don't understand why their powers aren't working; I mean they are both powerful beings, aren't they?" asked Ruby. Thaddeus responded, "Don't forget Ruby, when that awful day happened a few years ago, everyone's magic became drained, that is why we've had to practice too often and so vigorously, just to maintain whatever energy we've had left. Something went awry when the Murk brother's parents were killed." "I can enlighten everyone about that," replied Herald, "Queen

Primrose told us that she was able to communicate with the goddess telepathically. She said that Isoldina told her that on that dreadful day, Dracha, the brother's mother placed a curse on the kingdom. Since she was dying when she performed the dark spell, she wasn't at her full potential and the incantation only succeeded to do half of what she bestowed. She tried to abolish everyone's powers, and erase our memories of that despairing day so that her sons could rule with Quagmire on their side, and our alliance with the dragons would be destroyed." Abruptly, Thaddeus turned pale and exclaimed in a pained voice, "Quickly, Raven is in danger!"

Raven wasn't expecting another attack so soon, she tried holding off the unexpected onslaught of vultures coming at her from every direction. Her sword was out, slashing violently as she used her telekinesis to throw whatever she could at the vile birds. "Aaaaaaah!" she screamed as one of the evil fowls clawed her arm. She was holding them off well enough, but she was getting tired. Just when she thought her arms would give out, a sword came flying though the air and took out one of the predators. Then she heard yelling and Noble was by her side in a flash. Thaddeus worked on healing her arm, while Radkiel turned into a red-tailed hawk, and Ruby, surprising herself, turned into a great-horned owl. Radkiel whooped his approval at his young protégé, for a quick moment, and then signaled her to follow his lead.

Taking her left wing high, Ruby gouged the eyes of the first vulture that came near her. Kind of feeling a little disgusted and nauseous at the feat, she almost fell, but Radkiel flew to her side, and whispered, "Good job, you'll get used to it, don't forget, they're the bad ones," and she flew back up. Ornatia let out a battle cry and she and the other warriors took down the rest of the formidable creatures. Once everyone caught their breath, Radkiel said, "We've wasted enough time. They are producing these minions to help them, and we do not know how many there are, so we are at a disadvantage." Ruby ran to her sister and cried, "Are you okay, I missed you so much!" Thaddeus said, "She will be fine, a little sore, but fine." "Thank you," Raven said to the feeler, gratefully. Thaddeus smiled and walked away to let the sisters catch up for a moment. "I didn't know you could turn into an owl," Raven said in surprise. "I didn't either," remarked Ruby, just as shocked. They giggled for a moment and then got serious, "Our father was born a prince," Ruby whispered. "I figured as much," Raven whispered back. "But how did you…." Ruby didn't get to finish her sentence as Stark spoke in a loud voice, "We can all see how dire our situation is. Let's decide here and now how we will proceed as time is of the essence." Everyone except for Herald, gathered together to project their strategies.

The owl stood behind Isoldina as Magpie and the brothers stormed the filthy hole in the earth where the wizard and goddess were being held. Isoldina pretended to be weak as she whispered to Sagacity to do the same, not that he wasn't already. "What sorcery are you up to!" demanded the crusty old witch. Sounding despaired, Isoldina replied, "As I am weak, and powerless at this time, what magic could I conjure?" Swiftly, Herald flew out from behind the goddess and pushed her aside, he threw sea salt at the old witch and held out a black candle made by the wickets, as he lit the flame with his wand, he chanted, with Isoldina, "We bind you Magpie, evil crone, you are powerless to harm others and all we have known, you shall cause no harm from this day forth, as we set a fire from this torch!" A cold wind started to swirl as the cowardly brothers ran and left their grandmother, to face her consequences alone, as the wizard and goddess kept up the incantation.

It was decided that half of them would go after the Murk brothers and Quagmire, and the other half would hunt for the dragon's egg and Onyx. Knowing that it would be more to their advantage if they had the missing stone and egg, in order to conquer the evil dragon and gain all their powers back, they didn't want to take the chance of Quagmire's henchmen finding the mystical items first. Just as the vast group was about to separate, Gregor shouted, "Look!" as he pointed to the sky. Everyone cheered as they saw the big eagle with Isoldina held in one wing, and Sagacity sitting weakly on its back. When they landed, everyone bowed low. Isoldina, with tears in her eyes, admonished, "Please get up, I owe you all so much, most of all, an apology, do not bow to me." Willow was the first to approach the goddess as Thaddeus and the other feelers grabbed Sagacity to attend to his health. "You can still bow to me," the old wizard joked, in a raspy voice. They all erupted into laughter, and whooped, "All hail Sagacity!" The goddess took Willow's hands into her own, "I am so sorry my petty jealousy…." Willow interrupted her, "Please…I never knew you were in love with Edrical, I didn't know his past then." "I know you didn't," Isoldina whispered, "we were both so young, can we put that behind us?" Willow smiled, and hugged the goddess. Adorna said, "Let's get our old friends nourished and rested…" Stark stood by and smiled, making eye contact for a moment with Isoldina. "Ah, I almost forgot, forgive me for interrupting," said Herald, as he pointed his wand toward the ground, "Revealous, Appearance!" Magpie, tied up in black binding rope, clunked to the ground, to everyone's astonishment.

"Master, master!" the excited voices of the Murk brothers rang through Quagmire's sensitive internal ears. His scales quivered in annoyance at the interruption of his nap.

"Well!" snarled the impatient beast. "We found it, we found it!" 'You found what you infuriating idiots!" Nefari held out a glimmering blue egg, and almost dropped it as Querd slapped him on the back in admiration. Gritting his sharp teeth, the dragon hissed, "Well done, but if you drop it, you worthless slug, all will be lost, and without the other egg, this one is useless!" "Now," Quagmire tried to calm his voice, "Where did you find it, and where is Magpie?" The brothers glanced at each other in fear. How would they explain their grandmother's disappearance?

Back at the potions shop, everyone got ready to storm Murk Island. They left Raven, Noble, Herald, and a few warriors to guard the trident, and the frozen Magpie back at the Shadowstone home. The fairies and Kerina went to the forest to retrieve the dragon egg from the Dotted Elm. As the others waited for them to return with the egg, they checked their supplies, and Gregor exclaimed, "Uh oh!" Radkiel turned around, "What is it now?" "I still have Pappa gnome's telescope!" Radkiel grinned, "Young Gregor, when the Telli is finished with us you'll know about it. " "Okay then," replied Gregor, as he checked his backpack. Ruby said, "I just fed Boon and the baby mum, are we taking them with us?" "Daffilda and Kerina, as well as the wickets are staying behind," said Stark, "I think you should leave the mum with them." "She does have special powers," smiled

Ruby, looking at the now napping mum. "All the better reason to leave her here," replied Adorna, "We need magical beings everywhere. We don't know when another attack will come. If our powers weren't weakened by the curse of Dracha, we would be more cognizant of our senses. We are more powerful in large numbers because we can pool whatever magic we still have, together."

Nefari and Querd were preparing Quagmire's army for battle. Querd had escaped from Shimrock Mountain, and was back with his brother. Before Magpie was bound, she had conjured up a horde of foul troops to swarm the kingdom, and kept them hidden in the depths of the old volcano. Now they were gnashing their jaws in anticipation of causing destruction, which is what they were programmed to do. The brothers knew that this was their last chance to avenge their parent's deaths, and takeover the kingdom. Quagmire bellowed from his lair, "Are they ready!"

Raven was pacing the floor in the disheveled living room of her once beautiful home. Everyone did their best to help clean up the mess left by Sludge and the other vultures earlier, before they left for the potions shop. Noble broke into her thoughts when he came into the living room, "You haven't eaten much today, dear lady," he said sounding concerned. Raven looked at him and smiled wanly, noticing he didn't sound like himself, but she couldn't put her finger on what was bothering her. "What do you have there," asked Raven. "I picked some berries," he said, "You have to eat something." The young witch's stomach growled. She didn't realize how hungry she was, and she grabbed a bunch of the luscious looking berries and popped them into her mouth. "We should see if the guards would like some…" Noble grabbed her arm before she could go into the bedroom, and then the young witch started to feel funny. Before she passed out she looked at the young wizard and was horrified to see Querd holding her, then all went black.

Once Phinnia handed the egg to Adorna, she said, "I'm concerned about the color of the egg, its changing." "She's right!" exclaimed Ruby, "It's darker." Harmonia replied, "That's not a good sign, it means the other egg was found, and it wasn't by one of us." "Are we ready?" called out Stark?" "Not so fast," replied Willow, "we have a problem. The egg is turning dark, which means the other one was found, probably by the Murk brothers. Like Adorna said before, we are more powerful if we stay together. I do not think it would be a good idea to separate into two groups now." "I agree," said Thaddeus, "They are coming for us." Unexpectedly, Noble bolted into the room, "Help, I went out back, just for a moment, and I was struck down, I cannot wake up Raven, or the guards, and…and, I couldn't find the old witch!" Filling with rage, Stark yelled,

"Send a boy to do men's work!" Radkiel jumped in between them, "None of this nonsense, let's go!" Adorna and Serena stayed at the shop with Harmonia, and the rest raced off to the Shadowstone home. It was eerily quiet when they arrived there. Radkiel, Stark and Herald went ahead, and motioned for the others to stay quiet. When they didn't hear anything, Radkiel threw open the door and saw Raven on the now battered couch. "She's in here," he yelled. Willow and Adorna rushed over to the fallen teen. Raven moaned and Willow felt her forehead, "Shhhhh, it's, going to be okay, we're all here." Adorna picked up a goblet that was on the ground, noticing the spilled liquid. She sniffed the inside of the goblet and looked at Willow. Willow grabbed Adorna's arm in alarm. "Adorna said, "She'll be fine, its only slumber berries, probably a lot of them, infused into a juice." Willow let out a big breath, "Slumber berries?" Harmonia said, "Yes, enough to put her into a deep sleep. The brothers aren't as stupid as they seem. They know they need Raven and Ruby alive to complete their mission."

"This sounds more like Magpie, than those dimwits," replied Stark angrily. "Magpie!" Ruby and Gregor both shouted. Herald, Ruby, and Gregor bolted into the bedroom. Magpie was gone, and so was the trident.

Now that Quagmire had gained some strength back, he was able to climb out of his lair. He was grinning as he held one of the eggs that he knew held his brother or sister. Once they acquired the third egg, his siblings would be born, and he would no longer feel alone. Then he could raise them as he pleased, and use their powers to his advantage. The trident was finally in his possession, but the last stone was missing, and those two imbeciles couldn't find it. Could it be that it was found by his enemies and stored somewhere for safe keeping, but where, and where was the other egg? He felt the heat rise in his leathery face as his anger escalated into rage. He thumped his tail loudly and thundered, "Nefari, Querd, I'm ready!"

Magpie having a few tricks up her sleeve yet, knew she only had a little time left before Quagmire's temper would get the better of him, so she had to act fast. After Nefari had morphed into that dullard, Noble, she was able to escape the binding with a spell she taught Nefari years ago. Luckily her idiot grandson got it right, and actually had the remnants of the spell reversal. "Well," she mused, "He *is* the smarter of the two." Once the teen witch and the guards were asleep, Magpie and Nefari had conjured up a spell to break the protection charm that was safeguarding the trident. All they needed was something from the three witches, Willow, Raven and Ruby. Raven was easy, Nefari cut off a small piece of her beautiful black hair.

From Ruby they took one of the precious dolls, lying on her bed, and from Willow, a few drops of the perfume, from the bottle on her dresser. Winding the hair around the doll, and dripping the perfume onto it, the two evil sorcerers held onto the doll and whispered, "We call to thee that the trident be free, all in the name of the witch's tree, all combined by the power of the three!" Over and over they repeated the phrase until the ornate box shattered open. They held their ears at the loud explosion, and then beamed when they saw the trident glowing in all its glory. Grabbing it quickly, Magpie said to her Nefari, "Quickly, we have to return to the Island, before Quagmire's patience runs out!"

Willow looked around her once beautiful home and sighed. Thaddeus and Harmonia were tending to Raven and the fallen guards, as the others took up different tasks such as, setting up guard stations around the house, surveying the damage, and cleaning up the best they could.

Callioth, having just come from the forest said, "Crizal was generous with the amount of sap from the tree she gave me. We can start making some healing elixirs." Serena thanked Callioth and said, "Let's go to the kitchen and get started," she looked at Willow for approval, and her friend nodded. Kerina followed behind Callioth with a small army of wickets. The colorful troll like creatures brought a bounty of magical candles with them. "I had to leave some of my people behind on Wickardia," said Kerina, "I…" Adorna put her hand up, "No need to explain dear friend, each land in the kingdom, will have guardians left behind to protect them, we cannot take any chances of losing control of another one." Kerina nodded, and took a white healing candle made with bilberry and lilacs, to Raven's room. The sweet scented candle had a calming effect, which everyone needed at the moment. Ornatia, the captain of the guards, after setting up her soldiers around the home, came in and said, "Sagacity should be with the king and queen by now, and the goddess told me to tell you she would return soon. She had to go to Shimrock Mountain to check on things there and acquire some essentials she'll need here." All of the elders nodded, and Radkiel replied, "Okay, so each land has a witch or wizard on it and an assembly to defend it?" "For now," replied Ornatia, "Unless they are needed…" Without warning, there was a loud crash on the roof, and everyone took a stance. Raven jumped up off her bed, and screamed, "They are here!" In a flash, Ornatia and Herald bounded outside, followed by Radkiel, Stark, and Gregor. With one blow of his tail, Quagmire had the ground shaking uncontrollably. Adorna and the others held up their wands. Magpie shot a fireball at Adorna, but missed as the swordswoman rolled onto the ground out of the way. Willow shouted, "Quagmire, your fight is with me; do not destroy our land, a land that you were born unto!" Stark leaped to his sister's side, and stepped in front of her. Quagmire flicked his wicked tongue at the corners of his mouth, and raged on," You, and that diluted wizard of a husband of yours stole my siblings!" he thundered angrily. Ruby, her temper rising yelled, "You leave my father out of this, you foul breathed lizard!" Querd raised his wand and pointed it at Ruby, but Gregor was too quick for him and shot the brother with a bolt from his wand, hitting him in the shoulder, and stunning him. "Akkk!" yelled Querd. Appearing out of nowhere Isoldina yelled, "Quagmire, you were not born for this, you were supposed to be born with your siblings and brought up in peace and harmony, to live on dragoness." The dragon shook his ugly head, and pointed at Willow, "That witch, killed my mother, and stole the other eggs!" he hissed. "Not true," continued the green goddess, Iniquitis was not your mother that was an illusion perpetrated by her!" She pointed her want toward Magpie. Magpie, flicked her wand, and the goddess held up her hand to deflect the assault. For a second, the dragon looked confused, but then he bellowed, "Lies!" and he roared angrily. Querd nervously tapped his wand in the air and hit Raven's cape which went on fire. Noble ripped it off of her, and he and Raven both cast a bolt at Querd who was hit in the arm and screamed. He leaped behind a rock and moaned in pain. "Quagmire listen," demanded Isoldina, "Dracha and Xenos killed your mother." Magpie tried to shoot a bolt at the goddesses' mouth to quiet her, but Stark threw his shield up and blocked the attack. The goddess continued, "Your mother was a beautiful dragon by the name of Eragonia, she was the last of her kind, and felt safe here. She was protected by the kingdom, after your father was killed by the Elder Murks for not conforming to their ideals. You were trained by Iniquitous to be evil, she was Magpie's other daughter." Everyone looked shocked at this revelation. Nefari was at Quagmire's ear, "Master should we release the goblins yet?" The dragon shook him off, "All in good time," he whispered sounding annoyed and perplexed at the same time. Magpie took this moment to flick her wand toward Willow who was caught off guard. The bolt hit her wrist and she dropped her wand, and she cried out. Radkiel caught her as she fell to her knees. Ruby's blood was boiling and the heat was rising to her eyes, she could no longer control it, and flames shot out toward Magpie. The old witch tried to block the fire, but Raven used her telekinesis to remove the boulder that Magpie tried to hide behind. Querd, not waiting for approval, motioned for the goblin soldiers to move in. Everyone was fighting now. Balls of fire and lightning bolts flashed simultaneously, lighting up the darkened, cloudy sky. Isoldina knew she had to try to reason with Quagmire, she felt that if he knew the truth, he could repent and become whole again, not that Willow and the girls would forgive him for killing Edrical. Willing herself to fly up to the dragon, while the others battled Magpie's army, she spoke to Quagmire in a gentle voice, as she sprinkled remembrance dust in the dragon's face, and he sneezed as it went up his nostrils, "Try to remember," she coaxed in a soothing voice, "Your beautiful mother, hatched three eggs. Iniquitous stole the eggs and hid them except for you. She kept you to turn you evil, and hate all that is good. Her goal was to turn your siblings evil too, and take over the kingdom. She didn't care about you or your family. She, Magpie, and the brother's evil parents all wanted the kingdom for themselves. Iniquitous was jealous of the king and queen. Remember, Remember!" Quagmire's head felt heavy for a moment as he vaguely recalled a sweet voice singing to him. Then a foggy vision of a great beautiful blue dragon flashed before him, and he heard himself whimper. Shaking his head violently, he roared and pointed one of his legs at Nefari, "You! You lied to me!"

"Master?" Nefari shook his head nervously and sprinted over to his brother, who was howling in pain. Magpie was seething as she realized Quagmire was starting to believe the goddess's words, and her rouse was about to be revealed. Instantaneously, there was a loud clap of thunder, and everyone stopped mid- battle and watched, mouth agape, as Magpie rose up in a flash of light and was spinning around in the sky. When the spinning stopped, she slowly came down to the ground, her long black feathered cloak and hood draped around her. Her eyes were red, and although her face appeared younger, she still was ugly with wickedness. "Adorna gasped, "Iniquitous!" "I, I thought she was dead!" exclaimed Raven. "We all did!" replied Stark.

Iniquitous chortled a deep mirthless laugh, "Simpletons," she wailed, "I have yet to claim these lands!" Then Nefari yelled in disbelief, "Grandmother?" "No you fool!" cried the sorceress; I killed that old hag years ago!" Now Isoldina yelled, "So you pretended to be Magpie all this time, lying in wait for the right time to strike!" "Iniquitous screamed, "You will all bow to me, and I will be queen of Equonicous!" Suddenly there was a fluorescent haze and a loud whoosh, as a portal opened and Sagacity bolted through. "That will never happen," came the outburst from the old wizard. "Where is the trident?" Sagacity continued. "Is this what you're looking for?" teased the malevolent sorceress. Iniquitous pulled the trident from behind her robe.

Everyone gaped at the brilliance of the glowing metal. Meanwhile, Ornatia and her soldiers were battling the goblin army. Quagmire, who was beginning to believe the green goddess, raised his tail, and wiped out the grotesque goblins. At that, Iniquitous turned her head toward him, "Ah, so now you betray me?" She screamed venomously.

"You lied to me!" roared back the betrayed dragon. "Oh, did I hurt your feelings?" she laughed uproariously. "Are you turning into a sniveling dolt like that weakling, Edrical?" Raven, pointed her wand at Iniquitous, "Don't you dare, don't you dare speak of my father that way, he was a great wizard!" Stark pushed Raven's arm down and stood in front of her. The black hearted sorceress narrowed her eyes, "That imbecile was ruining my agenda with his puritan ways, always preaching of peace and goodness. No one was ever good to me, I'm glad I killed him!" A stunned hush spread suddenly as everyone realized it wasn't Quagmire who destroyed Edrical. Sagacity flew up and blasted Iniquitous with a jolt and she ducked as she sent one back. Raven exclaimed, "Ruby, your ring!"

She was so full of anger and hatred at the moment that Ruby did not realize her ring was glowing. Suddenly she was being pulled toward Iniquitous. "Nooooo," she screamed. Raven grabbed onto her sister, but the force was so powerful, it pulled her right along with Ruby.

Raven put a protective arm around her sister as they were pulled toward the evil sorceress, who was now fighting with all of the elders. Iniquitous did not realize the trident had slipped from her robe. The trident was now airborne and heading toward the sisters. Willow yelled and Iniquitous now saw what was happening. "Noooooo!" she screeched as she sent a fireball at the sisters. Radkiel turned himself into a raven and flew up to block the attack from the girls. He then sent a bolt at Iniquitous. Directly, the trident crashed into the girls and Raven whispered to her sister, "Your ring, the missing stone is in it!" Ruby, shocked at this revelation almost dropped the precious ring after quickly taking it off. The ring immediately stuck to the trident and Raven grabbed it. Both girls started to fall and Herald, turning into an eagle swooped them up and carried them safely to the ground. While the other elders were trying to fight off Iniquitous, The goddess restored the onyx to the trident. Iniquitous grew larger and larger as rage boiled within her. Without hesitation, now that the trident was complete, Willow, Raven and Ruby all grabbed onto the trident, and pointed it at Iniquitous. They fell back as the stream of electricity shot out of the weapon, but each held on tightly as the sparks flew at the immoral witch. Screaming, not so much in pain, as to the thought of being defeated, Iniquitous cried out before she perished, "This is not the end!" as she gurgled her last breath, and vaporized out of existence. Nefari and Querd took this moment to try to sneak away, but were caught by Ornatia and placed under arrest. Instantaneously, the sky cleared up and turned a bright blue. Phinnia, whose wings were full of soot, brought over the dragon's egg she was lovingly protecting, and placed it in front of the green goddess. Quagmire placed down the other egg he was hiding under his wing. Callioth pointed to Quagmire, "Look, he's turning!" As everyone watched, the dragon's skin went from dark and dusky to a bright cerulean blue. A big tear fell out of his eye and hit Gregor right on the head. "Yuck!" the teen expressed loudly. Daffilda exclaimed, "My goodness, the eggs are hatching!" Everyone watched in awe as the tiny dragons hatched.

Daffilda flew down with a basket, and placed the babies carefully into it. One was red and the other was purple. While everyone was admiring the new additions to the kingdom an owl hurriedly flew by and landed on Starks shoulder. There was a note in its claw. "It's from the king and queen," said Stark excitedly, "Our dear friends, we've been told by Pappa gnome that Ralliant has magically been restored, and the curse was lifted. Murk Island is no more!" The whoops and hollering were deafening as everyone shouted until their throats were sore.

"What's going to happen to the Murk brothers," asked Ruby. "They are being transported to the castle dungeon," smiled Sagacity as Willow hugged her two girls. They were all exhausted and hungry from the draining fight. Kerina spoke up, "Good news everyone, Crizal had said that once we won the battle, we were all invited to the Dotted Elm for a feast." "How did she know we'd win?" asked Gregor."

Kerina smirked, and shrugged her shoulders, "She had faith in her heart."

* * *

The next day, although still tired, everyone assembled into the forest and took their seats in the lush garden behind the Dotted Elm. There were beautiful flowers and candles everywhere, as well as the scent of fragrant lilacs. Everyone stood up as the bride came down the aisle and stood next to her groom. "My dearly beloved," started Sagacity, "we are gathered here on this beautiful day to witness the joining together of Radkiel and Adorna in holy matrimony…."

"Finally," whispered Daffilda. Phinnia shushed her but nodded in agreement. Isoldina was sitting next to Stark, holding her hand, and was glowing. "*Maybe I have another chance at love after all*," she thought happily. Pappa gnome and Gerlinda were also there and he retrieved Telli, after thanking Gregor for taking good care of her. Ruby was sad to learn that the little mum she'd become so fond of would have to be returned to the mountain, but Pappa and the green goddess assured her she could go and visit the little creature whenever she wanted.

"Just remember to bring some raspberry jelly biscuits!" Gerlinda giggled. After the ceremony; everyone celebrated not only the wedding, but their valiant victory the day before. Sagacity had offered Quagmire the courtesy of changing his name, but the grateful dragon decided to keep it as a reminder of his past and how indebted he was to the green goddess and his new friends in Equonicous. Sagacity decided to nickname him Mire, due to the king and queen's admiration of him reforming himself so quickly. It turned out that Mire had two sisters, and he had his wings full so to speak, as he raised them with the help of the fairies. Phinnia and Daffilda each named one, Phinnia named the purple one Amethyst, and Daffilda named the red one Starblaze.

Quagmire approved of the names, and was honored by the fairies' suggestions. Since Ralliant was restored, some of the inhabitants of Shimrock Mountain decided to go back to the land they once occupied. Isoldina created a tunnel so that if anyone decided to return to the mountain or just wanted to visit, they would have easier access.

The king and queen were happy to be reunited with Isoldina. Apologies for misunderstandings and stubbornness went all around. Herald went back to his post at the castle as did Noble, but not before asking Raven to be his girl. She blushed when he asked her to wear a ring he made especially for her, out of precious metal and an emerald in honor of her birthstone. Everyone pitched in to restore the Shadowstone home. They could have done it with magic, now that everyone's powers were restored, but Willow and the girls didn't want it that way. Edrical had built it from his own hand, and in honor of him, that's what they did. They also did the same with Serena's shop. Now that everything was back in order, Willow sighed as she watched her two beautiful daughters from the kitchen window, giggling in the garden as they practiced their magic. "For once," she thought, "All was right with the world."

The end... for now.

Acknowledgments

I'd like to thank my husband Tommy for putting up with my shenanigans and having patience as I test my writing ideas with him. To my wonderful children, Charissa and James Hemmer, you are the lights of my life, thank you for being who you are. I'd like to thank my dad, Sam Serio, who encourages me, and always supports my writing. Thank you to my sister Stacey Dufrene, who always gives good advice, makes me laugh, and lets me vent.

Special thanks to Maureen Cutajar and Jeanine Henning, two of the most talented people I know, I appreciate all of your wonderful work and for helping my characters come to life.

Last but definitely not least, thank you dear readers, I hope you enjoy this book as much as I enjoyed writing it, thank you.

About the Author

Alisa Guttadauro was born in Staten Island, New York. She developed a love for creative writing in middle school, and is an avid reader herself. Alisa enjoys spending time with her family, and going fishing with her husband, Tommy. They're newly adopted cat, Gus, loves to sit nearby while Alisa is at her laptop writing. Alisa is now working on Book 2 of *The Sisters of Dragoness.*

Made in the USA
Middletown, DE
21 February 2020